# WEST SIDE STORY

began on the Broadway stage and was immediately recognized as one of the most creative musical productions of the twentieth century. Its success as a motion picture was equally spectacular.

A classical story with a modern setting, it still stands as one of the major contributions of the American theater.

# WEST SIDE STORY

### A Novelization by
## IRVING SHULMAN

A novelization of the Broadway musical "West Side Story"
**BASED ON A CONCEPTION OF JEROME ROBBINS**
**Book by Arthur Laurents • Music by Leonard Bernstein •
Lyrics by Stephen Sondheim • Entire original production
directed and choreographed by Jerome Robbins**

PUBLISHED BY POCKET BOOKS NEW YORK

Another *Original* publication of POCKET BOOKS

POCKET BOOKS, a division of Simon & Schuster, Inc.
1230 Avenue of the Americas, New York, N.Y. 10020

ISBN: 0-671-50448-7

First Pocket Books printing November 1967

42   41   40   39   38   37   36   35   34

POCKET and colophon are trademarks of
Simon & Schuster, Inc.

Printed in the U.S.A.

# WEST SIDE STORY

# • CHAPTER ONE •

Riff Lorton looked at the wristwatch he had rolled off a drunk the week before, saw it was about nine o'clock, and groaned because most of the night was still ahead. Once daylight-saving time was in effect, the action had to start later, after it was really dark. But all day he had been feeling restless, itching and aching to get started, to get the Jets off their ass and into action.

It was all right for juniors like Baby-John to hang around and wait for orders, but nightly he had to show the Jets that he could keep them as busy and as important as Tony had when that missing person was planning their scene.

There were a couple of things they could do. They could move over to Central Park and look for a drunk they could roll because there were a couple of men in the Jets who needed watches. Or they could prowl the bushes until they found some jerk making it with his date and see if they could get into the act. They could even break up and walk through the Park singly with an exaggerated movement of hips, until one of them picked up some lousy fag to bust around before taking his wallet and watch.

No good, Riff decided, to each of these possibilities. Come dark, the Park was filled with cops who swung first and asked questions later. Any guy who was making out in the Park with a dame was probably raping her, so there could be trouble for the innocent bystander, and some of these faggots were surprising guys—longshoremen, truck drivers, judo experts, guys who looked like wrestlers—and tangling with them could mean a broken head. And you couldn't tell about the swishy-looking kind; they might be plainclothes cops, assigned to the pansy patrol. So the Park was out.

Of course there were the broads, but the Jets liked to lead up to that kind of action and if they picked up the girls now, they'd be stuck with them for the rest of the night; and the way Graziella hung onto him, she was going to make him into an old man before his time.

For a real bright, gone chick, she was getting some awful stupid ideas about getting married, and doing more and more yakking about how more kids their age were getting married every year. For crying out loud! She had even shown him the section of the newspaper that listed the names and ages of all the people who had taken out marriage licenses, and plenty of the jerks were just eighteen.

No sir, Riff told himself, and he knew the other Jets would agree, he was satisfied to do their jazzing without getting married and the rest of that jazz.

"This is Action asking what's the action?" Riff

felt his lieutenant nudge him. "What are we going to do tonight to blacken the name of our fair city?"

Riff picked at his teeth with an I.D. card that listed his age as twenty-two. Of medium height with a square face and chin and hair cut very short so that nobody could get a grip on it in a fight, Riff's eyes were large, intelligent and well spaced above his nose which had been broken twice.

Like the other boys in the Jets, he wore the standard warm weather uniform: chino pants or jeans, tight T shirts to show his muscular development, and short black boots. Waiting on his decision, the Jets gathered around him as he leaned against the lamppost; eyes bright with anticipation, lips pressed into hard lines of cruelty, fingers tensing into talons, they shuffled nervously, as if anxious to break from the wire.

Riff looked over their heads, as he had done so many nights before, in the hope that he might see Tony coming down the block. Why Tony had kissed them off the way he did was something Riff couldn't understand, and he was beginning to suspect the gas about his mother Tony had given him. His own old lady, Action's, A-Rab's, Diesel's, Gee-Tar's, all of them had been threatened every day, but so far there hadn't been any funerals.

"Stop looking for the Polack," he heard Action say. "Tony doesn't want any part of us."

"You know what's your trouble?" Riff asked him.

Action took a backward step and knotted his hands together to make the knuckles crack. "Go ahead, tell me off."

"In your case, two heads aren't better than one."

Baby-John hooted. "Hey, that's all right, Riff. Somebody new must be writing your material." He ducked to avoid Action's hand, then skipped toward the curb. "All right, Action. I'm sorry I laughed."

"Do it again and you won't have time to be sorry," Action warned Baby-John and included the other members of the Jets.

In his own mind Action had never been convinced that Baby-John was the kind of recruit they needed. Tony, in sponsoring the kid, had pointed out that most of them had started hanging around the Jets when they were thirteen or fourteen, because a kid who wasn't in was definitely out and might as well make up his mind to stay off the street. But there were kids and kids, Action thought, and Baby-John—well that was a hell of a nickname for someone who had to be depended on to stay in there swinging with a tire iron when the combat got heavy and the going rough.

With increasing frequency Action had begun to wonder if he ought to challenge Riff for the leadership of the Jets. But if he did, and was successful, he would have to tell the Jets what to do, really lead them; this way he could beef about everything that was done and keep Riff on his toes to prove his leadership.

Because Riff had to work at being leader, the Jets were a close, well-knitted bunch and none of the white gangs on other blocks wanted to tangle with them. Even the dinges knew enough to keep out of the neighborhood. Only the PR's were around, more and more of them every day, and if the damned cops and the mayor and everyone else didn't have enough sense to do something about it, the Jets did.

Maybe, Action thought as he continued to rub his knuckles, the mayor might get around to giving them a medal; there would be a great ceremony, lots of speeches, plenty of booze and broads, and at the end when they were given the medals, would they surprise the creeps by telling them what to do with the medals, and how!

"I don't know," Diesel said, after he flipped erect from a handstand, "but this seems like the slowest night I can remember." He looked overhead at the stars, then at the street lights. "I've got no inspiration," he added. "And I'm not tired enough to lay down somewhere and sleep. All night movies, anyone?" he suggested.

"Knock it off," Riff said. "We'll take a walk and see what develops. You . . . you"—he pointed to Mouthpiece and Tiger—"keep your eyes peeled for trouble."

Shoulders squared, both thumbs hooked behind the heavy military buckle of his belt, moving with stiff exaggerated steps, Riff walked with both eyes fixed at some far point. Anyone in his way would have to move, because this was their turf.

Behind him, the Jets moved in twos and threes, with Baby-John walking as close to Riff as he dared, imitating him as much as he dared, and hoping no one would notice, especially Riff, that he too had his thumbs hooked behind his belt buckle. Now Action, A-Rab, Big Deal, Snowboy and Gee-Tar were also walking in this manner. It was meant to tell everyone that the Jets were on the prowl, ready to take on anyone for anything—you name it—and anyplace, right now.

In appearance, manner, determination, the Jets were indistinguishable from thousands of other gangs that roamed the boroughs, and the most frightening aspect was that they had no targets for their hatred. By look, word and deed—even thought—they hated everything and everyone in their path. Without direction. they roamed the city, bent on destruction. Nothing was safe because everyone and everything was their enemy. Therefore, with the viciousness of blind, brainless beasts, the Jets fell upon anything they came across.

Their victim or target could be a man with whom they had been friendly the day before, a boy or girl they had joked with minutes earlier, a storekeeper who had always allowed them credit, a vacant building with a window yet unbroken. Dedicated to blind destruction, incapable of evaluating people and institutions, the gangs destroyed, and when they found no one else to destroy, they turned upon each other.

So the city became a battlefield of a thousand streets, ten thousand houses, roofs, cellars and alleys. The city became unsafe, and people walked and lived in terror.

Until the Puerto Ricans came upon the scene. Then the gangs had a purpose and target and the city became much safer for everyone—except the

PR's. They had come here without invitation so whatever disaster befell them was of their own doing.

Some thinking persons wondered what would happen if the PR's fled or were driven from the city. It was best not to delve too deeply or project too far. As things were, the gangs warred against the PR's, the PR's retaliated in kind. Optimistically, they might exterminate each other; and with this happy hope for the future, the city continued to conduct business as usual—and die.

Because the night was warm, people at the windows and on the stoops of the tenements saw the Jets, and only those who approved openly of their activities called out to the boys. Those who did not looked away or hid behind newspapers and handkerchiefs because the Jets meant trouble and in this crowded block there was more trouble than air, light, or hope. So why look for more?

On other streets there were other gangs that slept late in the day, stirred in the afternoon, and like prowling cats came fully alive at night to stalk the cellars, the alleys, the roofs, the streets of the crowded, decaying West Side of Manhattan.

There was no place to move, no place to go. It was twenty years since the Second World War had begun and ended, but housing that ordinary people could afford was still at a premium; and if a white man wanted to get out of his apartment there wasn't a landlord anywhere who wasn't delighted at the vacancy which he could immediately fill at an increase in rent.

And if he wanted to sub-divide three rooms into five, six, or even eight, he could fill every one of them with Puerto Ricans and really make himself a bundle so big and fat that he could spend most of any year in Florida or California. He need never see his buildings, his tenants, or do anything for the maintenance of halls, walls and roofs. If the building fell down the landlord could turn his property into a parking lot.

So in the end, even people who didn't like the Jets had to admit that the boys were doing something about saving what little was left to them of the neighborhood. If they didn't like the way the boys operated, at least the boys *did* something, which was more than could be said for the politicians and the gas they spouted downtown.

None of the politicians lived on the West Side; none of them had to fight for a little room, a little air to breathe; and if the city was unsafe, crowded, depressing, if more and more streets were becoming unsafe after dark, whose fault was it? Not one person in any of the tenements had ever been asked if he wanted the PR's admitted to the country. They had no voice in the decision but that didn't mean they didn't resent it. None of the newspapers spoke for the people on the West Side—only kids like the Jets, who used their voices and fists. It was best not to forget this.

Clicking their teeth, striking their heels hard, smirking from the corners of their mouths, the Jets crossed the street slowly, forcing automobiles to grind to a full halt. When one stupid driver leaned out of his car and ordered them to speed it up, Riff paused, glared, then walked toward the car with Action and Diesel behind him, and in frantic haste the man in the car rolled up his window and locked his doors. Like frightened fish in a bowl being attacked by a cat, the driver and the woman at his side could only squirm from side to side as the boys, with practiced coordination, spit all over the windshield and door windows before they stepped aside to release the car. As it passed they kicked the rear bumper, then howled with laughter, for this was another square-driven car they had kicked in the ass.

On the sidewalk again and pleased with himself, Action pointed out a middle-aged Puerto Rican man and woman as they came out of a small Puerto Rican grocery. They saw the boys, hesitated, looked at each other indecisively, and retreated toward the grocery. But they weren't going to get away that easy. Riff signaled, and Snowboy, who liked to think of himself as a commando, opened the grocery door to lob a small stink bomb into the crammed interior.

"What the hell," Snowboy said to Baby-John after he caught up with the Jets. "They live like pigs, so they shouldn't mind eating what smells like pigs."

Baby-John nodded sagely as he stored this information for future use. Not only had Riff and Action shown him how to handle snotty automobile drivers who thought they bought a street when they paid for a car, but Snowboy had handled the PR's in a way they wouldn't forget. And if they went home

and told their sons about it, and the sons came looking for the Jets, that was all right too, because any
PR who stepped onto Jet turf was really going to be
leaned on.

Belligerent, aching for contact, the Jets continued
their neighborhood prowl.

This was the second night they had surveyed the
scene without anything really happening, and Riff
knew the boys were becoming restless enough to turn
on him, which was what Action wanted. A leader
had to take care of his men, keep things popping all
the time, and the man who couldn't wasn't much of
a leader.

There was only one man Riff would have been
willing to turn the Jets over to, and as Riff thought of
Tony again he could only be bitter. Maybe that
was the trouble, Riff thought; he spent so much time
covering up for Tony that he didn't have enough
left over for the boys and the action they required.

Suddenly he heard Mouthpiece call out: three
PR's were across the street at nine o'clock. Turning
quickly on their heels, Riff and the boys started for
their targets. But the PR's, in their blue jackets with
the yellow trim that identified them as Sharks,
darted into a hallway and Riff cursed because it
was useless to follow them.

But if three Sharks were in the neighborhood
there might be others. Riff heard Action say that
he was going to make some mighty poor fish out
of them Sharks tonight, and as the Jets echoed this
fighting sentiment they began to look harder for the
enemy. About to turn a corner and break into two

squads, to cover more territory, Riff raised his hand in the signal that meant the worst kind of trouble: cops. Having acquired a wide experience of cops, they slowed to a walk and waited for the prowl car to pull a little ahead of them before it stopped.

Certain the Jets appeared innocent—out for a walk, nothing else—Riff was the first to approach the prowl car. Mouthpiece had ducked off because he carried the knives, two pairs of brass knuckles, and two lengths of bicycle chain that bulged one of his pockets. Riff smiled to himself as he saw how expertly Mouthpiece disappeared into a tenement basement. By using backyards and going up and down fire escapes, Mouthpiece would make it to the secret cellar bin which was their armory.

In an expert maneuver to block the cops from taking out after their ordnance man, Riff placed his hand on the car door to hold it shut and leaned forward to greet the plainclothesman and the uniformed cop at his side.

"Well, if it ain't Detective Schrank," Riff greeted the pleasant-faced man, now irritated, who attempted to open the door. "And Officer Krupke," he recognized the driver kept in the car on the other side by Action and Big Deal. "Now what brings you to this part of town?"

"Who was the guy who took off?" Schrank demanded. "And get your hand off the door before I break all your fingers."

Stepping back, Riff's eyes signaled Action to let the cops out of the car. "A fine way to greet some junior citizens anxious to live in peace with our representatives of law and order," Riff complained.

On the sidewalk Schrank took several hesitant steps as if to pursue the boy he had seen breaking off from the gang; but it would be impossible to find him now so Schrank exposed most of his teeth in a forced smile. Tall, beefy, powerfully built, with big hands that had broken their share of heads, he teetered on his heels as he stripped a stick of gum to place in his mouth. "Who took off in such a hurry?" he asked.

Riff made a big show of counting heads. "We are all present and accounted for. Now if you'll tell us to what good fortune we owe the pleasure of your company, we'll sing you two spirited choruses of our welcome song."

"It's no pleasure, and you're no company," Schrank said. He had been on the force for thirty years and his features had become hardened by experience and a philosophic fatalism that had made possible his survival. All people were rotten, was what Schrank believed, but the trouble makers had to be weeded out and beaten into submission.

"Anyone else moves off—the kids that I catch are gonna get it," he warned the Jets. "And don't look so snotty, A-Rab."

"Unfortunate me—it's my natural look," A-Rab protested. "If you know how I can look some other way . . ."

"Sure," Krupke interrupted rapidly. "Let's you and me step into a backyard someplace. Anything

I do to your face would have to be an improvement."

Schrank raised his hand to silence Krupke. "Which one of you threw a stink bomb into the *bodega* down the street?"

*"Bodega?"* Baby-John asked. "Please sir, if that's a dirty word, I am very young and innocent."

"I think you better get your ass home, kid," Schrank warned Baby-John. "You're goofy to be mixed up with these shape-up characters."

Snowboy draped a protective arm around Baby-John. He had used the last stink bomb on the grocery and was clean. "We're keeping him out of trouble, Detective Schrank, sir." He patted Baby-John's head, and the kid rolled his eyes in mock innocence. "We are keeping him away from evil companions."

"So you know nothing about the grocery?" Schrank ignored the ribbing to stick with the relevant issue.

Riff shook his head, then raised his right hand as if taking an oath. "We saw a couple of Sharks a couple of minutes ago," he suggested. "Maybe the grocery slob wouldn't pay protection or something. Now if you want to induct us as deputies and arm us with the weapons of the law—" he looked with longing at the heavy butt in Krupke's holster— "we'd be willing to serve without pay."

"Cut the comedy," Schrank said. "The Sharks didn't do it. The grocer said it wasn't a PR."

Big Deal exposed both palms as he shook his head sadly. "If it wasn't the PR's, and it certainly wasn't us, then I gotta come to a very sad conclusion. The outrage must have been done by a cop."

"Maybe two cops," Snowball said. "Renegades and traitors to their oaths of service."

"Correct," Big Deal agreed. "One to open the door, and the other to throw the bomb. Terrible, terrible," he clucked. "What are things coming to?"

"You're rubbing my back the wrong way," Schrank advised Big Deal. "Who did it? The guy who took off? Come on," he urged. "There's a difference between being a stool pigeon and cooperating with the law, or don't you rumblers know that?"

"We know the difference, sir," Riff looked from Schrank to Krupke. "You gentlemen taught us."

"It might interest you to know that we're saving up our scanty pennies to buy both of you gentlemen a suitable gift for giving us this knowledge," Snowboy declaimed with oratorical flourishes that doubled Baby-John with laughter. "It is the kind of knowledge designed to make us better citizens and without which we could have gone on living in blind ignorance. Then, how could we ever have done full justice to our civic responsibilities?"

After he raised a modest hand to still the applause, Snowboy bowed and took a backward step to put him beyond the reach of Krupke's nightstick.

"Listen to me, Riff," Schrank said, "and that goes for all your cruds." Moving quickly, Schrank fastened his right hand on Riff's shoulder and held him in a hard and painful grip. "The news I've got for you may come as a surprise." He tightened the grip and hoped the boy would wince. "You hoodlums don't own the streets."

"Never said we did." Despite the pain, Riff knew his voice was level and unconcerned.

"There's been too much raiding and bombing between you and the PR's. Now we've told it to them and we're telling it to you. Since you kids have to stay somewhere, we want you to be on your block and no place else. And you're not to block the sidewalk."

Action clapped his hands. "The word's official! We can't even go to work! Thank you, Detective Schrank!"

"Thanks for cueing me," Schrank pointed at Action, "because this is the appropriate time to mention the workhouse." No longer smiling, he chewed with a hard rotation of his jaws. "It's this way," he began, and the hard balling of his left fist warned the Jets to restrain their humor, "if I don't put down the roughhouse, keep this neighborhood clean and quiet, I'll wind up on a beat again, which means walking the same street with you, which I couldn't stand. Now I've got ambition, and you're going to have to play ball with my ambition. At least you're going to have to put up with it. So it's this way"— he tightened his fingers on Riff's shoulder and twisted to bring the defiant boy off balance—"I want you back on your block. I don't want you off your block. I don't want you looking for the Sharks or any other PR gang. I don't want you to do nothing that's going to bring them looking for you. You understand that, Riff? Goddamnit"—he shook the boy hard—"do you understand me?"

"I understand," Riff said. The pain was excruciating, numbing his shoulder, but he wasn't going to give the cop the satisfaction of knowing it. The Jets had to be proud of him, and he felt Tony would be, too. "You want us to behave like we always do. Peaceful."

"As for the rest of your trash," Schrank continued, "you can give them the message for me. If they don't do as I say, it means they want the crap beaten out of them. And my colleagues and me are ready, willing and anxious to oblige." The thrust of his hand made Riff stumble and fall against Action. "Get back to your block," Schrank repeated. "Krupke and me will be cruising it regularly because we want to tell you boys when it's bedtime."

There was no love, never had been, never could be, Schrank felt as Krupke and he walked backwards to the prowl car. Before he entered he moved his thumb to start the boys on their way, and from the corner of his eye could see that Krupke admired the way he had handled the situation. Krupke would remember this, would mention it; and it might be of some use to other cops who had enough of this sociology crap which preached that the underprivileged were often misunderstood.

He understood them all right, and if he had been able to get his hands on the boy who had thrown the stink bomb he would have rubbed his nose in it. Schrank exhaled soulfully and saw that Krupke nodded because the officer understood that both of them had thankless jobs—dangerous, too.

But a cop had no time to think of the danger. If he did, it meant that he was becoming frightened, and to stay on the force these days demanded an absolute indifference to fear. Jets and Sharks. They were only two of the gangs that infested the West Side. Sometimes it seemed to him there were more gangs than roaches. But gangs and roaches, both had to be squashed.

"Where to now?" Krupke asked.

Schrank sighed again. "To see if we can find the Sharks. I've got a little talking to do to Bernardo."

"Tough kid?" Krupke asked.

"He's just like the rest. Speaks English with an accent, but a good fist in his mouth is a language he's sure to understand. Everyone does."

They watched the Jets move along the street and hated the boys for their fighting strut—stiff legs, heels striking the pavement hard, shoulders rotating, thumbs hooked into their belts.

"Think we ought to go back to that grocery store and see if we can get a description of the kid?" Krupke suggested.

Schrank crinkled his nose. "No, I can't stand the stink."

"Of the bomb or the grocer?" Krupke asked.

Schrank's laugh was short and bitter. "No comment."

From the way his boys walked, the way they whistled, laughed and bragged, Riff knew the Jets felt they had gained a full victory, and over the cops at that. People had seen the cops talking to them, had seen the way he had stood up to punishment, and the word would get around to the PR's. Word might even get back to Tony, and it might bring him back to the Jets.

If Tony wanted to take over again it was all right with Riff. Smiling secretly to himself, Riff knew this would really tear up Action, but that was all right. Action had seen him take it from the dick—man, but the dirty bastard had a grip. He wanted to rub his aching shoulder but refused to do so because he wanted the Jets to believe that it hadn't hurt him a bit. No one could say he hadn't stood up to punishment like a leader.

The street clock above the barred windows of a credit jeweler told Riff it was almost ten o'clock. Things had happened mighty fast; and back at their corner the boys might spend another hour, talking it over, playing up their roles, telling each other what they were about to say to Schrank and Krupke, what they might have done if the lousy cops had swung even one punch. Then it would be eleven o'clock.

Still too early to go home, but not too early to go looking for the chicks. There were too many hours ahead until morning—hours of just nothing to do —and all that energy inside him ready, aching, to explode.

He had to see Tony, have another talk with him, beg him to come back. When Tony had been running the show every minute of every hour had been occupied, filled with things to do. True, at that time Tony and the other Jets had been busy battling to get title to the turf. They'd had to take on everyone to make the block their own, and Riff and the other boys had scars to prove that they had won the block and held it. There had been no one around who even thought of challenging them, no one until Bernardo, who was one of the first PR's to move into the block.

The other PR's lived all over the neighborhood, but Bernardo kept on bringing them down to the turf; and what he had in mind was very evident— to take over the block. If Bernardo and his Sharks could do this then all the white people would have to move out and it would be another victory for the PR's and their frabajaba talk. *Then* where would they go? Into the river?

Not for him, Riff swore. If anybody was going to live in the water it was going to be the Sharks. Damn spics! They never took a bath, kept coal in the bathtub; so kicking them into the river would be doing them a favor.

"Riff!"

Riff hunched his shoulders and refused to turn.

"Hey, Riff!" Anybodys was at his side. "What did Schrank want?"

Riff looked at the pale, thin, intense tomboy whose hair was cut almost in a butch. She had no breasts under her T shirt and her jeans were worn low because she also lacked hips. Dirty feet were stuffed into dirty tennis shoes, tied with broken laces, and as Baby-John ran forward to goose her,

Anybodys looped at him with a hard right round-house and the movement was that of a boy.

Failing to connect, she cursed Baby-John in a flat, gritty voice, then curled her tongue to spit at him.

"I'll get you later," she warned Baby-John. "What happened, Riff?"

"We had a talk."

"About what?" Anybodys asked.

"About you," Riff said. "Schrank asked if we wanted to get rid of you and we replied in the affirmative."

Anybodys reached for his arm but Riff shrugged himself free. "I don't believe you," she said. "You wouldn't say that about one of the Jets."

"You're not one of the Jets. But it's not for trying," Riff admitted.

"Then what is it?" Anybodys trotted at Riff's side and managed to hook her finger into his belt. "I'm willing to do what anybody else is."

"You mean that?" Riff asked her.

"Try me," she said.

"We're gonna look for the chicks," Riff said, loud enough for the boys to hear. "All of us. Even Baby-John. We're gonna get laid. What chick are you gonna promote?"

The sob torn from Anybodys' lips was drowned by a roar of laughter. Blindly, she struck out at Riff, but his left warded off her punch and Baby-John moved in to goose her again.

Tears spilled over to course down her dirty cheeks, and frustration made her search for a rock, a stick, a bottle, anything, but nothing came to hand; and ringed by the hooting Jets, she turned from them to dart into the traffic. She wove between wheels and fenders, oblivious of startled horn blasts, until she reached the other sidewalk.

"Not bad," Action complimented Riff. "Tony never got rid of her as quick as you did."

The season was spring, the month May, but the soft night was early summer. From where she sat on the tenement roof, Maria Nunez looked off toward Central Park and saw the bright windows and irregular patches of light. It had been a short climb from the fire escape up the ladder to the roof, and she had avoided unnecessary conversation with her father, mother, two uncles, two aunts, and several family friends, all crowded into the little kitchen with its one window.

Overhead the sky was prodigal with stars and thin, tenuous clouds had been torn apart by the passage of the moon. She had come to the roof at dusk to admire the tops of buildings less than a mile away, but separated by a greater distance than she had come a week before.

Night had come slowly to the city, to obliterate the form, thrust, and strength of the monoliths, to tone down the burnished metal and stone of intricate design, to erase the towers and bring patterns of color into tier after tier of windows. People lived differently in such rich, marvelous buildings, and with her chin supported by the palm of her hand, Maria wondered in what luxury they bathed and dressed. How different were the streets below;

not at all like Puerto Rico where the houses were little more than hovels without floors, without glass in the windows, and certainly without plumbing. Most of the streets were unpaved, without sidewalks, and poverty was everywhere.

When she had been met only the week before at the airport, she had had to blink and make certain that the man and woman running toward her with outstretched arms were her parents, for they appeared so much younger, more self-assured, even better dressed than she had last seen them two years before. At the time they had migrated to New York, it had been decided that she and her sisters would remain behind with relatives. Only Bernardo, her brother, would accompany them to New York until they could get themselves established.

Her father had frowned and not replied when she asked why Bernardo hadn't come to the airport. But she soon knew the reason. He was eighteen and handsome; but his eyes were too bitter, his mouth too tight, his voice too high, and every word he spoke dripped hatred of Americans.

They had more here in New York, more of everything, even of hatred; and to be rid of the latter Maria would have given up everything else and returned to Puerto Rico because she believed it was wrong to hate. She didn't want to hate when it was so much more wonderful, joyous, to love.

Maria yawned, stretched her arms and wondered if she ought to go to sleep. She might go down and study English grammar or practice speaking English with her father and try to remember that in this language verbs were placed differently in sentences. But the kitchen was filled with company and they were probably talking about San Juan and the little community they had once called home. Why had they left Puerto Rico? This they need not answer, for they had only to touch their pockets and look at the kitchen sink with its faucets.

Winking lights cut diagonally across the city, and Maria followed that flight. Was this plane coming from Puerto Rico? Was it returning to Puerto Rico? Again she was tempted to return to the kitchen, but everyone there would be speaking in Spanish, and if they spoke English it would sound like Spanish. She wanted to speak English as Americans did, with harsh consonants and clipped vowels and no music or lilt in their speech. She wanted so much to be an American.

Maria stood to stretch her arms and embrace the moon and stars. Yesterday she had been sixteen and her mother had kissed her many times as she exclaimed what a beautiful bride Maria would be. And Chino Martin, Bernardo's friend, had looked at her with eyes filled with love. Later he had spoken to Bernardo and to her parents about wanting to marry her. He was a steady boy and worked as an apprentice in a dress factory on Seventh Avenue; some day he would be a full-fledged union operator. Chino was good looking, very shy, much different from Bernardo.

Standing on her toes, moving about, Maria whirled and kissed her hands at the sky and the distant towers. If she married Chino her sisters would have more room because she and Chino would have a flat of their own. And if they made love, it would be more wonderful because they would have the privacy on the day they were married that her mother and father had not known for almost twenty years. Maria covered her face. She had to stop thinking such things, even when she was alone on the roof and in love with the world.

Did it include Chino Martin? She wasn't quite sure. Yes, she loved him as she loved everything in the world, but no more than that.

She heard the heavy metal door to the roof open and turned to see the dark shadow of a man. A startled flash of fear vanished at the sound of her name, and her respondent sigh of relief was loud enough to tell Bernardo she had recognized him.

"How come you're sitting on the roof alone?" Bernardo challenged his sister.

"Why not?" she asked him.

"Because it isn't safe," he said. "Not even if you were sitting up here with Anita."

"Why not?" Maria persisted in this question. "Isn't Anita your girl?"

"I guess so," Bernardo said. Resting against the parapet, he lit a cigarette, flicked the match toward the street, and watched the path of its descent. "It isn't safe to sit on a roof alone. There's too many bums in this neighborhood. If one of those Jets saw you sitting up here no telling what might happen."

Despite the night's warmth, Maria trembled. "Would one of them have done . . . that?"

"Without thinking twice," Bernardo replied, then dragged hard at the cigarette. "One of them threw a stink bomb into Guerra's grocery tonight. If I catch him he won't have any arms left."

"You know the boy who did it?"

"What's the difference? He was a Jet. The first one we catch is going to be the first one to get it. If they catch one of us, we get it."

"But why should it be this way?" Maria asked her brother. "Why should they hurt us?"

"Because they say we hurt them by coming here. You know what I'm going to do?"

"What?"

"Maybe tomorrow, I'm going down to Times Square with a couple of the boys—Pepe, Anxious, Toro, and Moose. And we're going into one of them souvenir stores."

"To rob it?" Maria was frightened.

Bernardo stroked his sister's cheek. "Of course not," he said. "Just to buy some iron statues of the Statue of Liberty. Some of them come about this long"—he indicated a measurement of about twelve inches—"and they'd be just about the right size for beating in the head of those Jets. You know what it says on the Statue of Liberty?" he challenged his sister.

"No," she replied. "Should I?"

"It says something about all the poor people coming here to find a better life. Well maybe it's true," Bernardo continued, "but the Jets don't believe it. So we got to beat it into their thick heads. And little Statues of Liberty seem just the right way to do it."

Maria stood to confront her brother. Eyes wide, her heart beating so hard it was frightening, she shook her head slowly as she fixed the knot of Bernardo's tie which had slipped to one side of his collar. Her brother was so good looking, but his mouth was too thin, and his eyes were like those of an animal she had once seen in a trap; they were fearful, but defiant in their hatred. His enmity was often unspoken, but more to be feared than noisy rage.

"Why must it be this way?" she said. "These people," she moved her arm to encompass the city, "I don't hate them."

"But they don't love you," Bernardo replied. "Look," he was impatient, "I don't want you on the roof alone."

Maria wiped at her eyes. "Not even with Chino?"

"Not even with Chino," her brother replied.

"But he likes me," she said. "Is it true really, that he spoke to mamma and pappa—about marrying me?"

"It's true," Bernardo embraced his sister and crushed her to him. "After you're a bride, you can be alone with Chino."

"Don't go anyplace by yourself," Bernardo warned again. "The lousy Americans think they're entitled to more than we are, and if they see a girl like you . . ." He paused, stepped back, cocked his head and looked at his sister. "Man, you are one sweet chick. Chino's a lucky fellow. By the way, Maria, you know that he loaned mamma and pappa the money for your fare? Even paid the fare for one of the kids? You know that?"

Maria bowed her head. "I know that. So I must work hard at my job to earn enough money to pay it back."

"But you like him?"

"Yes." Maria said.

Bernardo crushed the butt under his foot and removed a fresh cigarette from the pack. "How about loving him?"

"I don't know," Maria said. "But he's a nice boy."

"Let's get off the roof." Bernardo took his sister's hand. "The company's gone and you can go to sleep. By the way, I forgot to ask you. How do you like your new job?"

"I love it!" Maria clapped her hands. "Imagine, working in a bridal shop! The dresses, the veils, everything is so beautiful."

"You'll be the prettiest bride," Bernardo said to his sister. "The most beautiful of them all. When Chino sees you coming down the aisle it'll just knock him out. Maybe he's not like the other Sharks, because he's got a job and goes to work. But I wouldn't want any of the other Sharks for you." He opened the roof door for his sister and bowed gracefully. "*Si,* he'll make you a good husband, Maria. So you ought to try to fall in love with him."

"I'll try, Bernardo," she promised. "I'll try with all my heart. Are you going to sleep now too?"

"Later," Bernardo said. "I've got to see some of the boys."

"About what?" Maria asked. "To go fighting?"

Bernardo kissed his sister's cheek. "Just to talk things over." He was evasive.

"God go with you," she said.

"Sure," Bernardo replied. "I don't care if He comes along."

# • CHAPTER TWO •

For more than three weeks now the Jets had been ambushing Sharks and the Sharks had not chickened out. Riff had fought his way to the street from his own tenement hallway, and a paving black had missed Bernardo by inches.

Night after night the tempo was stepped up, until Schrank and Krupke were on the block every nightfall, searching for Riff and Bernardo and their boys. But the boys knew the neighborhood warren better than the police, and doubled up in a cramped dumb-waiter, on a cellar shelf inside a trunk, deep in a dark bin or under the steps of a tenement, the Jets and Sharks waited for the neighborhood to clear of cops. When this happened—it could be two, three, four in the morning—sniping began again, and each morning brought more casualties, more tension to the block.

The last four nights running, the Sharks had got the better of the Jets, had shown more ingenuity in their ambushes, but the Jets fought back. Mouthpiece had thrown another stink bomb into the grocery in the hope this would bring Bernardo and the Sharks out in full force, but Bernardo had refused. In retaliation, he had Pepe and Nibbles waylay Baby-John in an afternoon movie.

The point of an icepick had been pressed into Baby-John's back and he was warned not to cry out. Once they had him in the men's room, Nibbles crammed Baby-John's mouth full of toilet paper before they pushed him into a booth and clobbered him around. After they had half-drowned him in the toilet bowl, Pepe had nicked Baby-John's ear with the icepick and told him to take his brand back to the Jets with a message . . . the Sharks were willing to fight the Jets, but not willing to take it out on old people. If the chicken-livered Jets didn't cut it out, they were going to be gutted but good.

"That does it," Riff told the Jets. They were meeting in his flat because his mother and father were working overtime. "Nobody gets away with busting around Baby-John."

"I'm a casualty," Baby-John was proud.

"You're branded," A-Rab said. "Which sort of makes you PR property, I guess."

Riff pounded the table with the heavy end of

his spring knife. "Cut the chatter. You know the Shark that did it?" he asked Baby-John.

"One of them was Nibbles," Baby-John said. "But you know those dirty bastards all look alike. They said they gave me this for stink-bombing the store." Baby-John gingerly touched the lobe of his ear. "Are you guys going to let them get away with it?"

"We've had it," Riff was emphatic. "Now we really go to work. Answer the door, Diesel," he said because they had heard a knock.

Riff hoped that Tony would be at the door. For days he had been leaving messages for Tony in the letter-box, telling him how bad things were, how much he was needed. But it was Anybodys in the doorway, and she was able to slip into the kitchen under Diesel's arm.

"How come you didn't tell me about this meeting?" she challenged Riff.

"For chrissake, are you still around?" Action demanded. He rose from his chair which had been tilted against the wall and popped his lips in disgust; Anybodys gave him the creeps. "Want me to throw her out the window?" he asked Riff.

"Nobody's throwing anybody out," she said, and to prove it, she menaced them with a beer mug which she had broken so that the handle was retained and the rest was jagged glass. "Now who've I gotta mess up to prove I gotta right to be a Jet? Riff," she appealed, "how about me getting into the gang official?"

A-Rab held his nose as he hooted and pointed

at Anybodys. "How about the gang gettin' in . . . ahhh, who'd wanna?"

"You dirty rat!" Anybodys lunged at A-Rab. "I'm gonna carve you!"

Moving quickly, Riff clamped a mugging hold on Anybodys, disarmed her, and tossed the weapon toward the garbage can which stood near the sink. "The road, little lady, the road." Riff pushed her through the door which Tiger had opened. With the door locked and the chain in place, Riff turned again to his boys. "Are you guys in condition?"

"We're in condition," Action led the chorus.

"Good." Riff returned to the table and looked around him with pride because there wasn't a chicken in the outfit. "Now the way I see it," Riff began, "we hadda do a lot of fighting for this turf, and I'm not gonna stand by and see some greaseballs take it away from us. They're satisfied to hit and run, but that kinda fighting bugs me. Furthermore, I wanna get this over with. So we come to the conclusion. We take them on and clean them out in one all-out battle."

"All of us against all of them?" Action bounced to his feet and began to throw hard looping punches into the stomach of an imaginary opponent. "This is what I've been waiting for."

"Now you've got it," Riff was sharp. "But maybe them jokers don't want to do it with fists. Maybe they go for bottles or knives, or even to cool us with heaters."

Baby-John's eyes became very wide. "You mean

guns? Not that I'm afraid," he added quickly, "but guns? Where're we gonna get guns for everybody?"

"I'm just saying they might," Riff explained. "I'm just saying that if that's what they want, are we prepared to give it to them? I'm ready to finalize it anyway they want it. But I want to know your mood."

Diesel and Action were on their feet, shouting that they were ready to go, go, go. Mouthpiece and Gee-Tar made carving gestures at each other's faces. Big Deal stabbed at Snowboy to the heart, as Snowboy aimed a forefinger at A-Rab. They were playing at death, but ready for it; and as Action began to shout that he hadn't carved anyone in a long time but hadn't lost the knack, Baby-John's lips began to tremble. He touched his ear and the feel of dried blood no longer made him brave.

"I say let's fight them with fists, even with rocks," Baby-John said, "but no knives or guns. We don't have to fight the way greaseballs do." He wondered if his fear were evident. "If we don't fight them dirty and challenge them to fight us clean, that'll prove they're chicken if they don't fight as clean. Won't it?"

Diesel covered Baby-John's face with the palm of his right hand and pushed the kid aside. "What do you say, Riff?"

"This street's all we've got," Riff said. "It ain't much. You'd think nobody'd want it. But them PR's got other ideas. Nobody, but nobody's taking what's mine."

"You're speaking for all of us," Mouthpiece said.

By punching his right fist into his left palm, Riff acknowledged the backing of the Jets. "I want to hold our turf like we always did." Again he smacked his right fist hard, and was pleased that some of the others imitated him. "But if they say switch blades, I'm ready to use mine. And if carving our name all over them is the only way they'll get the message, this man is ready to deliver it."

Big Deal's laugh was loose and silly as he continued to make carving motions with both hands. Tiger disemboweled Snowboy, who clutched at his stomach as his knees melted under him. Action snapped his fingers so hard that it sounded like the rapid fire of a gun. Riff was pleased. The boys were behind him all the way. And as he cranked his right arm to imitate a whirling propeller, Baby-John began to run in circles and make bullet noises with his mouth.

"Okay," Riff gestured for the Jets to simmer down. "Since we're white and don't believe in taking unfair advantage of the enemy, and seeing that no other way comes to mind, I'm gonna have us call on the Sharks to send their war council to meet our war council and decide on weapons. But I'm taking the challenge to Bernardo personally."

No one disagreed with Riff, because as leader of the Jets this was one of his major responsibilities—probably the most important.

"But you gotta take a lieutenant," Snowboy suggested.

Action pushed Gee-Tar and Mouthpiece aside. "That's me, Riff."

"That's Tony," Riff contradicted Action. If Action hadn't said anything, Riff would have chosen him to go along. But Action had to be shown he wasn't the boss. "I'll go talk to him right now."

"Just a sec," Action blocked Riff. "Who needs Tony? I'm not for brown-nosing anybody. He walked out on us, so let's not turn him around."

Riff was deliberately patient, another characteristic of leadership. "We need every man we can get against the Sharks.'"

"Didn't you hear me, Riff?" Action continued to shake his head. "Or wasn't Tony speaking loud enough when he said goodbye?"

"Cut it, Action-boy," Riff said. "Don't tell me you've forgot that Tony and me, we started the Jets."

There was no disputing this fact and Action saw that he lacked active support. True, some of the boys felt as he did about Tony—goddamn hunkie —who just took off without any reason other than something about his old lady. But Riff was leader and fact was fact; Tony had started the Jets.

"Well, he acts like he's too good for us," Action continued to argue. "And if that's the way he feels, I wouldn't ask him if it meant saving my life."

"The Jets count more than any of us," Riff said. "That's one thing Tony will see."

"You're right," Baby-John said after he had made certain that he was far enough away from anyone so that getting pushed in the kisser wouldn't be his answer. "Tony's like the rest of us. He's proud of being a Jet."

Action spit at Baby-John. "Tony hasn't been around for more'n three-four months."

"What about the day we clobbered the Emeralds?" Snowboy asked.

"Yeah," A-Rab nodded. "We couldn't have done that without the Polish Panther."

Baby-John rubbed the back of his neck. "He saved this for me, all right."

"It's settled," Riff said to end the debate. "Tony goes with me to see Bernardo. He never walked out on any of us," he challenged Action, "and he feels about this turf like we do. I can guarantee that. Now, Action, any more questions?"

"Yeah," Action said. "When're you gonna get rollin'? I don't believe in letting PR's grow old peacefully."

"Which brings up a real question," A-Rab spoke loudly to get the attention of everyone. "Where're you gonna find Bernardo?" He stood on tiptoe, with his hand over his brow and searched for the leader of the Sharks. "I've got a report. I don't see him or," he sniffed, "smell'm."

"Simple," Riff sing-songed as he did a simple time step. "There's a dance at the center tonight. Right?"

"Right," the Jets chorused. "So we bite . . ."

". . . the Sharks," Riff picked up the patter. "Bernardo thinks he's quite a stepper, so he'll be there. And we'll be there with all our . . ."

"Might." Big Deal shut one eye as if in thought. "Seems to me I heard somewhere that the center's neutral territory and Schrank, Krupke, and company are there a lot. Unless you're thinking of changing that, Riff."

"We'll keep it that way for a while," Riff said. "But if Bernardo's there, I'm gonna challenge him. Now, it's gotta look like we're at the center for dancing and sociable sociability. So everybody get dressed up, and pull your zippers high."

Mouthpiece made shaving motions. "What time do we get there?"

"Between eight-thirty and ten," Riff said after a moment's deliberation. He looked at Action for his suggestion, and Action nodded. "Let's not all get there in one bunch," he added. "It's gotta look as if you're going to a dance, nothing more."

"That means we've got to bring dates?" Baby-John mourned.

"Sure," Action said. "You can take Anybodys."


As he darted through a tenement hallway, flipped over a fence to the next street and walked down its middle, Riff really felt that he was moving tall. Alone now, it was best to stay in the middle of the street where the danger from automobiles was less than the danger from the Sharks who could dart out of a hallway, clobber him one-two-three, and leave him on the sidewalk with his stomach stomped flat.

It was important that he get to the center ready to swing like a king and to show the other gangs at the dance that Riff Lorton was as good as Tony Wyzek, and that the gang hadn't fallen apart just because Tony had stepped away. Walking rapidly, snapping his fingers, Riff felt himself growing taller than the buildings, taller than anything, so tall that he could have punched his fist through a cloud and used it to wipe his shoes.

Time was going to drag now—yeah—until he got to the dance and put the challenge to Bernardo. He wondered if the PR would chicken out and leave them the turf without a battle. He hoped not. If this was what Bernardo planned, the only thing to do was stink-bomb his apartment. Hey, how about that? That would be one way of putting the challenge to the enemy—an idea Tony had once had—a thing that every gang on the West Side and everywhere in the city would have to admit was the coolest method of drawing the line they'd ever heard of. Man, that would really be bopping the enemy!

Tempted to return and see what the Jets thought of it, Riff realized that it was too late to round them up now for such a reckless gig. What they had already planned was dangerous enough; what he wanted to do could only mean a running, fighting attack, and retreat down the dark stairs of a tenement where they might be battling not only the Sharks but everyone else in the house.

The challenge at the center would do just as well; then, if Bernardo chickened, they could try the other. What a bunch—Riff glowed at the thought of the boys—everyone knew who they were and everyone stepped aside when they passed, which was the way it should be.

Soon, soon, the street would be theirs again, and every block that touched their street would belong to them, and every block that touched every block that touched their street would be—Riff broke into a run as he moved his right arm before him—theirs too. Property of the Jets, that's the way it would be. And Tony didn't know it yet, but he'd been chosen by Riff as the man who was going to help enlarge their world. What an honor he was giving the guy!

A block from Doc's pharmacy, Riff paused to draw breath and light a cigarette. Puffing slowly, he felt his heart action return to normal and judged his reflection in a store window. Satisfied that he didn't look excited, and certainly not worried, because this was the last thing he wanted Tony to see—that he was worried—Riff began to whistle.

A couple of minutes ago, he had been thinking as if on a jag; now he knew how things would shape up if Bernardo were at the center. Bernardo would accept the challenge, and Bernardo might go for switch blades, even guns. A week or so before Riff had run into a couple of the Musclers—a dinge gang that operated in Harlem—and seen how one of them had been cut from forehead to chin by a Shark.

If this rumble came off, it was going to be their big all-out effort. Whether Action or Diesel or anyone else knew this was unimportant, because *he* did, and Tony was going to be put wise to the knowledge.

Winking at himself, nodding sagely, with the corners of his lips turned down at his reflection in the glass, Riff told himself everything would be all right. The cigarette flicked over his shoulder and continuing to whistle easily, Riff entered Doc's drugstore with both hands raised to assure Doc—who glared at him suspiciously—that he was here on serious business and not to cop anything off a counter.

"Tony quit?" he asked and looked at the clock. It was five-thirty; damn, he didn't want to go to Tony's house.

"Tony's out back," Doc said. A slender man of less than medium height, Doc wore thick glasses that were forever slipping down his nose. His white coat was stained with sweat under the arms and the loose slippers he wore made his feet ache because they offered no support to his arches. Breathing deeply as he counted out pills to fill a prescription, Doc kept the number in his head. "What do you want to see him about?"

"That's for me to know and you to find out," Riff said as he pretended to pull a comb from a display rack on the counter. "I'm not going to steal nothing, Doc. Only your boy and my friend. How much are you paying him anyway?"

"That's for Tony and me to know and for you to find out. If you're really interested," Doc paused, "and sincere, I might be able to find you a job like Tony's. Then you'd know."

"Up yours," Riff said as he moved toward the rear door.

Behind the store was a little paved area enclosed by the walls of three buildings. In one corner were stacked cases of empties of various soft drinks and large glass bottles of distilled water in wooden crates. Against one wall were stacked cardboard display signs and a variety of dusty articles which Tony had cleared from the basement.

"We did it last week," Tony explained to Riff. "Doc decided that everything had to be saved until he went into the basement and almost broke his neck when he tripped over something. So now, we've hauled all this junk out again. You know what?" he asked Riff.

"What?" Riff asked dutifully.

"All of it's gonna go back," Tony said.

"Doesn't sound like important work to me," Riff observed.

Tony sighed deeply. "I can't do a hell of a lot more," he admitted, and was surprised that he could say this without shame. Christ, he wasn't any older than Riff, so why did he feel like a big brother or something? "I been thinking of going back to night school. What do you think?"

"I think you ought to have your head examined," Riff said and quickly raised a hand in a gesture of peace, because Tony's eyes had become dark. "Tony, listen, I'm here on really important business. We're going to the center tonight to look for Bernardo."

"Seems to me I heard *he's* looking for *you*." Tony wiped at his face because the day's oppressive heat hung heavy in the yard. "How about something cold?"

Riff shook his head. "I'm here for something cool. A man who's going to be at my side when I challenge Bernardo. Once and for all, we're going to lay it on the line."

Tony shook his head. "If you came to count me in, count me out."

"You're kidding," Riff said. "Hold it." Again he raised a hand to keep Tony from replying. "You're going to say you're not—and I'm gonna ask you why. So tell me?"

"Because it's so stupid, even I can see it," Tony replied. "Riff, listen . . ."

"I'm listening," Riff interrupted him. "But it ain't easy. Because it's *me* asking you, Tony." He tapped his friend's chest, then his own. "It's me, Riff, remember? Tony, for chrissake, stop pushing that garbage around! This is important!"

"Very important," Tony was ironic. "Planning to get your head broken. On you it won't be becoming."

Because he was frankly puzzled, even worried about his friend, Riff took a backward step to see Tony in better perspective. A couple of years ago they had sworn their friendship was womb to tomb, sperm to worm; now he couldn't reach Tony.

"What's with you?" Riff asked. "It's been a long time, man, our knowing each other. A long time, and I thought I knew your character. Boy," he shook his head slowly, "I thought I knew you like I know myself. I'm real disappointed in finding out different."

Tony laughed as he gently punched Riff's right shoulder. "So stop being disappointed. Stop suffering, little man."

"I'm not a little man!"

"So grow up." Tony was sharp. "Riff, I'd like to

finish up." He pointed to the cellar doors, thrown wide. "Maybe go to a beach someplace for a swim. You know, I've never been to a beach . . . How about it, Riff?" He was excited. "Let's go . . . to Rockaway! We can go swimming at night. How about it?"

"Knock it off," Riff said.

"I see," Tony replied. "You'd rather go play with the Jets. Okay, little man." He repeated this with emphasis. "Give my regards to the juveniles."

"The Jets are the greatest!" Riff shouted and kicked out the wood slats of a box to prove it. "The greatest!" He raised his voice even higher and looked up at the buildings to see if anyone dared challenge this boast.

"They were." Tony replied quietly.

"Are," Riff insisted. "You found something better?"

"Not yet."

"Then what the hell are you looking for?"

Tony thought for a moment. "I don't think you'd dig it."

Riff tapped his chest. "Try me, man. I'm very sharp. Go ahead."

It had come to Tony one night, alone, on the subway. It was a feeling of discontent at the nagging sense of inferiority that even leading the Jets couldn't erase. He was ignorant, knew nothing, and all the big-man-in-the-world talk wasn't going to change it. Sure he was cool, but so was a cake of ice, and what did it know? Nothing. He was ignorant. And the way he was going he'd always be ignorant. There had to be something more than this.

Many hours later that night, because he had ridden trains from Brooklyn to the Bronx, from the Bronx to Queens, and from Queens into Manhattan, he had returned to his block off Columbus Avenue and walked up the dark steps that smelled of every meal ever cooked in the house, every bottle of booze drunk there, every drop of sweat brought on by the summer, the salt of every tear wept in rage or despair, and sat on the roof until dawn.

That was his last night as a Jet, his last night as a leader. The next morning he had looked for a job and Doc had given him one in the drugstore. Frankly, he didn't know whether Doc had given him a job because it would be cheaper to have him on the payroll than to have God-knows-what done to the store; but he had been working now for four months and if the Jets were upset about it, his mother wasn't. And it was time, Tony thought with shame—also a new feeling—that he did something to make her happy.

Or was that too square? He dared not tell the Jets, he dared not admit to anyone to what emotional confusion his thinking had led him and the easiest way out was to brush off Riff, Ice, and Action, who had taken over the Jets.

"I'm speaking to you in confidence," Tony said.

Riff felt heartened. "Which means that we're still friends?"

"Right down the line." Tony smiled, then became serious. "I've been doing an awful lot of dreaming," he began. "I'm always standing someplace and reaching out for something."

"What're you reaching for?" Riff asked with a diplomatic show of interest.

"That's hard to say," Tony continued. "At first I thought it was going somewhere. Not a mile away or a hundred miles but thousands of miles. To places on the map."

"So join the navy," Riff scoffed, "if you want to get screwed and tattooed in every port. What's the production? You can get the same thing here and make believe it's a thousand miles away. You wanna see Chinks, go to Chinatown. You wanna see Africa, it's two-three subway stations up. You wanna see Italy, how the hell far is Mulberry Street? But if you want to see Puerto Rico, go to Puerto Rico. That's one thing I don't want to see around here."

Tony waved his hand to dismiss the narrowness of Riff's logic. "I don't have to go a thousand miles to find what I'm looking for—maybe. It could be right around the corner, outside the door." He pointed at one of the dark windows in the building that loomed overhead. "It could be right there."

Riff leaned back "What's up there?"

Tony's tongue felt swollen as it did when he dreamed. "I don't know." It was an effort to speak. "Some kind of kick, I guess. More than a kick," he continued, "but I don't know how to say it any other way."

"Are you becoming an addict?" Riff was horrified. "You listen to me!" he pointed at Tony. "If I ever find out that you . . ."

"Forget it," Tony reassured him. "I'm looking for something that will give me the same kick I used to get . . . out of being a Jet!"

Riff thought for a moment. "I get my kicks out of thinking that we're still buddies."

"We are," Tony said and reached for Riff's hand to shake it hard. For a moment they Indian-wrestled, then with a quick flick, Tony jerked Riff off balance. "Beat'cha again."

"And glad to be beaten, so long as it's by you. The kick comes from people, Tony," Riff explained.

"Yeah," Tony agreed. "I got a lift out of seeing you. But if you'd come here with A-Rab, Diesel, any of the other guys"—he shook his head—"I don't know. I'm thinking, right now, Riff, about being a Jet." Again he shook his head. "Sorry, no kick."

"Boy, you sort of forgot the facts of life." In his disgust Riff stove in the side of another crate. "Kick or no kick, without a gang to call your own, boy, you're an orphan. Around here you need a gang more than you need your old man and old lady. I'm not saying anything about *your* mother," Riff added hastily, "not after the way she's treated me. But Tony, facts is facts. If you don't belong, you're nowhere, and belonging to the Jets puts you on top of everywhere."

It was impossible for Tony to deny the sincerity of Riff's appeal, impossible to erase the history of years together, back to back. In bright, clear, and focused tableaux, scene after scene crowded into the first rank of Tony's memory, kicked there by his conscience. Still, he did not want to give in.

"Riff, I've had it." He wished that he had spoken more emphatically, but his throat felt clogged. "All the way."

"The trouble is large, Tony," Riff replied, for he had noticed the weakness of his friend's reply. It was an effort not to appear exhilarated, but he made it successfully. "The Sharks bite hard, Tony. We gotta stop them now or get out of here." He paused for Tony to appreciate how desperate the situation was before stretching a hand to plead for help. "I never asked the time of day from a clock, but I'm asking you. It's help I need, Tony. All in capital letters. We want to see you at the center tonight. They're having a dance."

Tony turned away. "I can't make it."

"I already told the boys you'd be there," Riff replied.

Angry at being committed without being asked, Tony was tempted to throw a hard left at his friend. Then he realized why Riff had done it. Because Riff still thought of Tony as his friend, his best friend. Maybe he didn't feel the same way about Riff, but that didn't excuse his letting Riff down. Not only Riff, but all the Jets, the whole neighborhood.

He didn't like Bernardo and the Sharks. No one had invited them to come here and if the battle was on, there was no point in asking who was responsible. It was on, that's what mattered, and Riff had appealed to him not as a Jet, but as a friend.

The night he had walked away from the Jets he had told them that he wanted Riff to take over. He had put Riff out front. Now it was his responsibility, no getting around that, to keep Riff walking ahead of everyone else.

Tony grinned. "I didn't want to buy what you're selling, but I didn't know what kind of a pitchman I was up against."

"Ten o'clock?" Riff asked.

"Ten it is," Tony replied. "You know something? I've got a feeling I'm gonna live to regret this."

Throwing jabs, Riff shadow-boxed. "Who knows? Maybe what you're waitin' for'll be twitchin' at the dance! Man, when was the last time you had it?" he roared. "See you!"

A bank of clouds moved overhead, shutting out the sun. Tony felt trapped in the hot, narrow yard as dismal as the walls and dark windows above him. He cursed himself for not having been firmer, for not having turned Riff down. Once and for all he should have made it clear for even the stupidest to see.

He should have carried through on his plan to go to the beach. And as he sat on the shore, the taste of salt on his lips, his fingers digging into the sand and his eyes on the stars, something might have happened. The magic thing that he was groping for might have cannonballed right out of the sky.

What would it be? Another beach? A waterfall? Thousands of birds flying in formation? Jet trails in the sky? A trapeze slung from the moon? Might it be a girl? Why not?

The clouds had passed across the sky, darker blue now because the hot, weary day was surrendering to the dusk. He could hear Doc calling, telling him it was quitting time for hired help but not for bosses, and that whatever hadn't been done could wait until the morning. Only he should be sure to lock the cellar doors, then come in for a cold drink.

"It's going to be hotter tonight," Doc said from the doorway where he fanned himself with an old issue of a pharmaceutical magazine. "And hotter tomorrow."

"I guess so," Tony agreed.

"I'm going to an air-conditioned movie after I close up early, about nine," Doc said. "If you'd like to have a sandwich with me, a bottle of beer, you could be my guest. Or if there's a girl you'd like to take along, I could give you the pass and buy a ticket . . ."

"I'd like to, Doc," Tony said. "But I gotta date."

"Riff and you and two girls?"

"Not exactly," Tony said. "I'm meeting him at the center. There's a dance."

"So, I can't blame you for turning me down," Doc said after a shrug. "But how can you dance on a hot night? So you won't be alone, that answers my question. I'll see you in the morning?"

"In the morning." Tony knelt to snap the lock on the cellar door. "Take it easy, Doc. I'll pass by about nine and help you close the shutters over the windows."

"Thanks," Doc said. "Some world, when you gotta have iron shutters over store windows."

"It's the PR's," Tony said.

"And not your friend Riff—and the other raff?" Doc was ironic. "All right, Tony, I'll see you tomorrow and don't worry about the shutters. I'll manage. But take care of yourself tonight."

# • CHAPTER THREE •

The bridal shop was just large enough to accommodate three sewing machines, three dress dummies, a small table for cutting fabric, and a little dressing booth. A sign had been lettered on the window announcing to passers-by that English was spoken within. Señora Mantanios, the middle-aged widow who owned the shop, had thought that the sign might attract trade that was not Puerto Rican. But during the one week the sign had been there, neatly lettered in gold and large enough for anyone to read, she had not been called upon to use one word of English.

Disgusted that people could be so intolerant, the Señora had left early to bathe and change her clothes. Two friends—amateur matchmakers—were bringing a man to call, a gentleman who had been widowed a respectable number of years. The night offered no promise of relief from the heat and she wanted to have pitchers of tea, coffee, and lemonade in her refrigerator; also some wine and beer.

For several anguished moments she had hesitated to leave the shop in the hands of Anita Palacio. Anita was a good enough seamstress and well trained in Puerto Rico, but she was running wild in New York. Anita had explained that she wanted to remain behind only to help Maria Nunez alter a dress she was going to wear to a dance that night. The dance was in the center that had once been a church, and it all sounded respectable enough.

After many admonitions that the girls were to make certain both doors were securely locked, and the iron shutter drawn and secured across the front window—to keep the Anglos from stealing the dress on the dummy in the window—the Señora departed.

She hurried toward the tenement in which she lived, not because she was late, but to minimize the amount of time she had to spend on the streets. Much too often the Señora had been a target for the mouths of dirty, filthy boys. They were blondes, redheads, some with freckles, all of them Irish, Polish, God-knew-what-else, and why He had created these countries and their people was a mystery she would never understand.

Both doors of the store locked securely, blinds drawn, Maria came out of the dressing booth in her white dress. "Do you think you can make the alterations by tonight?" she asked Anita.

Anita nodded because she had several pins in her mouth. Almost eighteen, with dark, savage eyes that became brighter in the dark, Anita was an inch or two taller than Maria and several inches fuller across the breasts, hips, and seat. Bernardo swore that his girl had to be melted down and poured into the dresses she wore, that they fitted her like a second skin—molded, man, molded.

Anita wore her hair long, loose, and wild, and used eye-liner even during the day. Her lips were heavily lipsticked and enlarged, so that they always appeared to be full blown with passion. During the day she worked in flat-heeled slippers, but wisps of plastic shoes with three-and-a-half-inch heels stood beside the sewing machine.

"Now will you please hold still?" Anita cautioned in Spanish.

"Talk with me in English," Maria replied.

"If you want to speak English, you have to think in English. But I like to think in Spanish," she rolled her eyes expressively, "because that's the nicest language for thinking about love. But please, right now, I want you to stand still."

Maria reached up to unfasten a button at the collar and turn under the high neckline. Her communion dress was of soft, white rayon with eyelet embroidery at the neck, at the cuffs of the three-quarter-length sleeves, and the hem. Around the waist had been a white sash which Anita had promised to re-place by something dark red or blue and Maria could wear a complementing band in her hair.

But the neckline was too high and the sleeves too long; still, if she had to make a choice between the sleeves and the neckline, she wanted something done to the neck.

Maria reached for a pair of scissors. "I want you to fix the neck," she said. "Make it like the dresses you wear."

"You're going to make me swallow pins," Anita said. She was working with a ruler to mark the new hem of the dress, which would be slightly below the knees. If Maria had been someone else, not Bernardo's sister, she would have recommended a length two inches above the knees, but that would have made Bernardo furious, and not in the way she looked forward to that night.

Man, there were times when he became so angry his eyes were filled with fire, so hot they did all sorts of wonderful things to her. Then she helped him get rid of the anger and they were both happy in their exhaustion, and Bernardo spoke to her in the low-est, sweetest whispers.

"You've got to stand still," she warned Maria, "otherwise you're liable to get a pin you know where."

"You'll do something about the neck?"

"The neck's all right. All the girls I know should have such lovely necks."

"I'm talking about this dress," Maria protested. "Two, three inches what difference does it make?"

"Too much difference," Anita snapped and rolled her eyes expressively to make Maria laugh.

"You're making this dress over for me to dance in," the younger girl argued. "To dance in," she repeated. "It's no longer for kneeling in front of an altar."

Anita placed another pin in the hem. "With those boys you can start in dancing and end up kneeling, begging them to take you to the altar."

"If not three inches or two inches—one inch." Maria showed how little this was between her thumb and forefinger. "One little, little inch."

"Bernardo made me promise," Anita sighed. From her place on the floor, she could see the graceful slenderness of Maria's legs. Lucky girl . . . she would never have to shave her legs and be forever committed to using creams and lotions to keep the skin soft. "It's not me," she explained to Maria. "Bernardo made me promise to take care of you. And that includes altering the dress."

"Bernardo made you promise," Maria scoffed. "I've been here one month now, and still he walks me in the morning to the shop. And if Chino can't meet me, Bernardo comes to walk me home. Sew all day and sit all night," he complained. "Just what I did in Puerto Rico."

"You were a little girl in Puerto Rico and you're not much older here."

"Is that so?" Maria said. "If I'm a little girl, how come it's been arranged for me to marry Chino?"

"Oh, that's nothing," Anita explained. "You're

old enough to get married, but not old enough to wear a low neckline."

"But I'll be old enough not to wear any clothes," Maria continued, then hid her face because she had to blush and laugh at the same time. "You mustn't tell anyone I said such a thing, not even Chino."

"Certainly not Chino," Anita said. "How is it"— she fluttered her hands—"does your heart do that even when you look at him?"

Maria shook her head. "When I look at Chino nothing happens."

Anita groaned as she got to her feet. "What did you expect to happen?"

"I don't know." Maria was serious. "Something, I guess. He's nice, but . . . he's nice." She took several steps to stand before the mirror and see how long the dress would be. It was an inch below her knees, but enough of her legs showed to please her. Now if she could only get Anita to do something about the neck, and one way to do it was to keep Anita talking about other things. "What happens when you look at Bernardo?"

"I can't look," Anita replied. "He fills my eyes with stars until I'm blind. Then it happens."

"I see," Maria said. "That's why you go to the movies and can't tell anyone what the picture was. Yes," she continued, "now I understand what happens when you and 'Nardo sit in the balcony. I wonder if I should tell my mother and father why you know nothing about the movies?"

Anita fastened her fingers on the collar of the dress. "I'll rip it to shreds," she warned.

"Perhaps if you could manage to lower the neck . . ." Maria suggested, her eyes assuring Anita that she would never reveal so personal a secret.

"Next year," Anita tried to look severe but had to smile. "There's time enough." For a moment her eyes were sad. "Believe me."

Maria pouted and raised the dress a bit; there, her knees showed, that would have been a better length. "Next year I'll be married and if I'm wearing a dress who'll care how long it is?"

"All right," Anita raised both hands in surrender. "How much do you want the neck lowered?"

"Down to here," Maria touched her breastbone, then frowned at herself in the mirror. "I hate this dress!"

"Then don't wear it and don't come to the dance," Anita said, and hoped Maria would take the suggestion.

Quite certain that no matter how she altered the dress, 'Nardo would find fault with it, Anita wondered why she had to put up with something like this when she could have been at home lying in a tub filled with bubblebath. She would have raised her legs and arms as if in a striptease, thinking the most delicious, immoral thoughts, which was a good way to get rid of the sadness and envy over Maria. Tell the truth—she told herself—you might've been like 'Nardo's sister, but never looked it. Dress Maria in robes and she would look like the Madonna.

"Don't come?" Maria was shocked. "You or no one else is going to keep me away. My mother gave me her permission." Again she deliberated by tapping a fingertip against her lower lip. "Couldn't we dye the dress red? You looked so wonderful in your red dress."

"No we could not!" Anita was firm. "Maria, please. There is enough to do just to get the dress ready . . ."

"White is for babies," Maria complained. "I'll be the only one there in a white . . ."

". . . if you're going to be there, it's going to be in a white dress," Anita said. "So make up your mind, please."

"The white dress," Maria capitulated, "with the neckline lowered just a little bit." She insisted upon this. Suddenly she grasped Anita around the waist and kissed the older girl's cheek. "You're so good, Anita, and I love you."

The hard knocking on the front door gave Anita an excuse to free herself and avoid the shameful folly of tears. Possibly if she had been lying in the tub she might have thought about something else: how much time had passed since she had been like Maria. But she never had been, not from the first moment she had become aware that boys were different.

She opened the door, her smile warm and sensuous as she saw Bernardo, with Chino behind him. The tip of her tongue flicked between her lips, and Bernardo gave her a quick wink before he shifted his features into blankness.

With his shoulder he gestured for Chino to come into the store and step aside as Anita locked the door. Hands clasped awkwardly behind his back, Chino bobbed his head and spoke hardly above a whisper as he greeted both girls, but looked only at Maria, still posing in the white dress.

"How'd things go today?" Bernardo asked, after he permitted Anita to kiss his cheek.

"Pretty good," Anita said. "A couple of customers came in. And one of them said she wished her son was marrying a girl as pretty as either of us."

"As pretty as you," Maria corrected Anita.

"I heard it otherwise," Anita said. "Chino, why are you leaning against the door?" She pointed to a chair. "Sit there."

"This is a shop for ladies," Chino explained. His nervous fingers plucked at his shirt collar and he fanned himself with his light straw hat. "Some day outside," he observed, because weather was the only thing he could discuss with girls and not feel awkward.

"Forget about the day," Maria ordered him. "It's this night that's important, 'Nardo." She turned to her brother. "It's most important that I have a wonderful time at the dancing tonight."

"Why?" Bernardo asked. He tried to catch Chino's eye, to urge him to say something, even one of the things he had suggested on the way to the store, but Chino insisted upon staring at his shoes. "What's so important about tonight?"

Whirling, pirouetting before the three-paneled mirror, so that her reflection was multiplied again and again, until, from where Anita stood, it appeared as if a full ballet dressed in white was interpreting a dance of innocence, Maria pointed and skipped toward her brother who smiled now as he had in the old days. Tonight was going to be so wonderful, Maria thought. that she had to imitate Anita, so she kissed Chino on the cheek. His skin was very warm, very nice, and nothing more.

"Because tonight is the real beginning of my life as a young lady of America!" Maria sang. "Chino" —she grasped his hands—"I want to dance tonight. And dance and dance and dance! Even when there is not playing music."

## • *CHAPTER FOUR* •

Several years earlier, two congregations of a religious denomination had combined, and the older of the two churches on the West Side, the one more in need of repair, had been put up for sale. For almost a year the church had stood vacant, its windows a natural target, until the religious denomination had offered the building to the city authorities if they could find use for it. The gift had been accepted and the church converted into a community center. A variety of clubs for boys, girls, and adults had been started and the center creaked along, never quite successful enough to instill pride in the social and community workers assigned to it, but never an outright failure.

Although the community center had been open to everyone, its primary purpose was to get boys and girls off the streets and to offer them supervised play and instruction. The program was intelligent and well meaning, but it suffered from one major flaw. It was available to everyone in the neighborhood, including the Puerto Ricans.

Once it was understood that the Puerto Ricans were welcome, the original and older inhabitants of the neighborhood began to avoid the center and it was almost impossible to get their children to use the facilities. And then the Puerto Rican families stayed away too because they did not want to use the center if it were boycotted by Anglos.

Most of the time the clubrooms were empty, the books and games remained on the shelves, the basketball court had no one on it, and the social workers congregated in an office to brood over cups of coffee and mourn their choice of career. It was a rotten, thankless job.

On this June night, however, Murray Benowitz was happy and confident of the future. As in the past, he had publicized this dance without optimism, had encouraged the youth workers to do what they could about getting kids to attend, but had urged them not to be disappointed.

If this was a bitter, jaundiced point of view, it

was founded in experience. As do many of those who make a career of social work, Murray Benowitz had viewed the world through rose-colored glasses and had seen it as the best of all possible places. Now he knew differently; the world was gray, grim and bleak. But he had to smile to keep from crying, to smile when the kids destroyed equipment, scrawled obscenities on the walls, and derided him for being a square. They called him Glad Hand, but he took it and strangely enough, still managed to think of them by their proper names.

Since eight o'clock that night, teen-agers had been swarming into the center, and Murray had had to call on two additional workers to come and help him. Standing by the record player he glanced at the fireproofed crepe-paper decorations strung gaily above the dance floor.

There were good records to be played. The punch was cold. There were reserve sacks of ice cubes and plenty of cups and napkins.

Although both Sharks and Jets had shown up, no fights had started. Murray had shivered with apprehension but the Sharks moved off to one side of the dance floor, the Jets to the other, and each group danced in competition—as if there were a wall between them.

Well, Murray thought, it was a beginning. Soon he and the other workers would attempt to get both groups together, but boys and girls were still coming to the dance, and he was far too busy.

Moving along, calling out to boys and girls whose names he remembered, stopping to chat and managing to laugh when he was greeted as Glad Hand, Murray decided not to notice that the dancing was becoming wilder and more primitive. He had always correlated mixed dancing with sexual aberration. Later, if he could ever gain the confidence of these neighborhood kids—prove that he was their friend and wanted to help them—he might speak to the district supervisor about the need for a dancing teacher.

Murray's eyes blinked behind his glasses as he looked toward the door and saw the Sharks gathered near it. He recognized Bernardo, whose girl friend was wearing a bright red dress, and crossed to welcome personally one of the boys he most hoped to influence.

From the corner of his eye, he saw a stirring where the Jets were congregated, so he moved more quickly. He reached the door just as Riff, Action and Tony Wyzek appeared.

This was really going to be a night! Over the weekend he was going to write a full and glowing report to let them know downtown that at last, at long last, he felt optimistic about the progress he was making.

Years of hard experience told Murray that the air around him was becoming charged as the Sharks grouped themselves behind Bernardo and the Jets formed a phalanx behind Riff, Action, and Tony.

Could he have heard wrong, Murray wondered? Doc had told him Tony Wyzek was working steadily and had dropped all association with the Jets. Still, the boy might be a throwback, who had become lonesome for his old associates and their dog-eat-dog attitude.

He had to think rapidly, speak quickly, because it looked as if both gangs were going to tangle right then and there. He saw that two of the girls with the Jets had removed their shoes, ready to use the high heels as weapons.

"All right, boys and girls." Murray made himself beam as he waved both hands for recognition. "May I have your attention, please? Attention!"

He waved a hand at a police officer who looked in through the door and signaled the uniformed man that everything was all right, under control, no trouble anticipated.

"That's fine," Murray approved the response to his request, which, he knew, had been considerably helped by the uniform. "It's sure a fine turnout tonight. The best we've had in a long time. But the night's young, only a little after ten and we want to make it better." He paused for breath, and compelled himself not to hear the boys and girls as they mocked his professional heartiness. "I hope you're having a good time?"

"You said it, Glad Hand!" a girl shouted.

"Fine, but I've noticed that you've been dancing on different parts of the floor, as if the Grand Canyon were between you."

"Whee," a boy called as he postured with a hand on his hip, "do you want the girls to dance with the girls? And the boys with the boys?"

"I want you to dance with each other," Murray

gestured in the direction of the Sharks and Jets. "So you can get to know each other."

"We know them stink-bomb merchants!" a Shark called out.

Murray raised his hands again. "Let's not talk about the past," he suggested. "We're having a good time tonight. As we get to know each other, we're going to have an even better one. So let's start with a few get-together dances. You'll form two circles. Boys on the outside. Girls on the inside."

"Hey, Glad Hand, where will you be?" Snowboy yelled.

Murray forced himself to laugh. "All right. We're going to start the record and the boys will move in one direction and the girls in another . . ."

"Dir-ty!" someone shouted.

"Two circles, kids." He swelled his voice so it could be heard above the lubricous, sly laughter. "Then when the music stops, each boy dances with the girl opposite him. Okay? Okay. Two circles, kids."

Cheeks and forehead beaded with perspiration, glasses misted, he could still see that they did not move, that the Jets and Sharks continued to glare at each other.

The highly rouged, elaborately hair-styled girls in tight dresses, their breasts made prominent by nature or design, also signaled their challenges. The silence became heavier, more pregnant, and with an explosive sigh of relief that made him ashamed, Murray saw that the first policeman had returned with another, whom he recognized as Officer Krupke.

He waved, called out to Krupke, and as the Jets and Sharks saw the policeman staring hostilely at them, they moved to form circles around their own girls. Bernardo stood opposite Anita; Riff paired himself off with Graziella, who snapped her fingers impatiently for the music to start, because she loved to dance and they were wasting time.

But this was not what Murray wanted, and again he explained. He looked at Krupke who barked that the instructions seemed simple enough for anyone to follow, so how about it?

There was no way to defy orders, so the proper circles were formed, the record was started, and Murray clapped his hands as the boys and girls began to move in opposite directions. "That's it, kids. Keep the ball rolling. Round she goes and where she stops, nobody knows! All right, here we go!"

Murray shouted and signaled one of the other social workers to stop the record. He blinked, opened his eyes wide and was disappointed. Although the circles had stopped, so that some of the Jets were opposite girls who had been escorted to the dance by Sharks, they only glared at each other, until Riff, with a manifest expression of disgust, turned away from the Shark girl in front of him and beckoned for Graziella to come to his side.

It was a gratuitous insult and outraged the Sharks the more because a Jet had thought of it first. Trembling with rage at this public humiliation, Bernardo snapped his fingers for Anita, the gangs broke apart, the girls following them.

Murray signaled for another record to be played immediately, and sighed with relief when the music of a hot, wild mambo filled the room. This was the kind of music to calm them, which was strange, until he began to think in anthropological terms. Music did occasionally intoxicate savages, and that's what was needed now. Something to get them drunk on music, so they couldn't think of hating. Later, when the dance ended, the Jets and Sharks would leave and then it would no longer be his responsibility.

Murray Benowitz shuddered. He wondered if Krupke would mind driving him to the subway station and seeing him safely on a train for home? What a way to earn a living!

From the moment he had arrived at the dance, Tony had felt out of place. He hadn't brought a date and everyone there was paired off. And when he saw Bernardo and the Sharks, Riff and the Jets, they all seemed like foreigners. If he moved toward the door, no one would notice and he could get away. If Riff were stupid enough to challenge Bernardo, that was his business.

Then he saw the girl in the white dress standing against the wall. And as he saw her, she saw him, and any thought he had of leaving was gone. As if he were being led, Tony Wyzek approached Maria Nunez, looked into her dark eyes, stretched out his hands, and was led by her into another land.

The mambo had ended and a lighter, slower record had been placed on the turntable. As Tony drifted onto the dance floor, he gently clasped her fingers and looked down at her heart-shaped face, her liquid brown eyes, her lovely mouth just touched with lipstick. He nodded to approve of her dress which was white, beautiful, so different from anything worn by the other girls.

His fingers barely touched her back. Her touch on his shoulder was light, fragile; when he moved her through a turn and his hand pressed more firmly, she shuddered and moved as if to leave him, so Tony tightened his fingers only for a moment, then relaxed them.

There was nothing to fear, he told the girl. Never having been in this land before, he knew it well. It was a gentle land of green fields, warm winds, brilliant birds and perfumed flowers; no matter that they walked on clouds, they would not fall. Although he heard the music, it was as if from a distance.

Maria felt that her heart might burst. Were the lights above them dimmed so that she could not see this Anglo boy with whom she danced? And why wasn't she frightened of him? Why didn't he look, act, speak, as Bernardo said the Anglos did?

The night was hot, she felt perspiration trickle down the small of her back, but the fingers of this boy were so cool, and he danced so easily, without pressing against her, without trying to "sock it in," which was how Bernardo described Anglo dancing. But she had seen how Bernardo danced with Anita, how all the Sharks danced with their girls, so they were no different from the Jets.

"You're not thinking I'm someone else?" she heard him ask. It was a good voice, very shy.

Maria shook her head. "I know you're not."

"Or that we've met before?" Tony asked instead of shouting with joy that the girl wasn't going to leave him. He was certain of that now. This was as it had to be in this land: people who entered together remained there together, forever.

"I know we have not," Maria replied. "I . . . I'm glad I came to this dance."

"So am I. You know, I'm was just leaving. Then I saw you, and I got the message."

She was puzzled. "What message, please?"

Thinking was one thing, expressing it another. He wet his lips, then began slowly. "I don't know. Last couple of months I've been sort of going around asking myself who I am? What I was doing? Where was I going? Was something big ever going to happen to me? Sometimes I get so low my . . . excuse me," he stammered. "I mean, I'd feel so blue, wondering if I wasn't kidding myself about the thing that was gonna happen. Do you understand what I'm getting at?"

"I think so." Maria was grave. What wonderful eyes this boy had. She had never heard it explained better by nyone. "Of course I understand," she added, hesitated, and decided to continue. "I felt that way on the airplane."

"I've never been in a plane," he said. "It must be wonderful."

Conscious that the music had ended, Tony was glad that they had danced toward a corner where there was a bench. "You know," he began, after they were seated, "you seem to know what I'm gonna say even before I say it." Her fingers rested on the edge of the bench, and he covered them with his hand. "They're cold," he said.

"Yours too." Gently she raised her free hand to touch his cheek, as she had done earlier that evening to Chino. The skin was rougher, no warmer, but her fingertips felt as if they had touched a live electric wire. "Your cheek is warm."

Tony dared to touch her chin. "You're warm too."

"But of course," Maria smiled. "They are the same. And it is warm. It is—"

"Humid?" he supplied the word and was pleased that she nodded.

"Yes," she thanked him. "But still it is not the warm of weather."

"You know what I just saw when you said that? Fireworks," he continued, after she nodded. "Great big pinwheels and rockets. But no sound, only lights. There"—his forefinger traced a trajectory—"see them?"

"Yes," she said. "They are beautiful."

"You're not kidding? Not saying it to make me feel foolish? You really see them?"

Maria traced a cross above her heart. "I have not yet learned how to joke that way, and now . . ."

". . . yes?"

"I think I never will."

The rockets were rising, joining together to explode in hearts and stars before they descended in a waterfall of light. Impulsively, because her hand was almost at his mouth, Tony moved his lips to kiss her palm. And as he did, he felt her tremble.

He leaned forward to smell the lovely sachet of her hair and the fragrance of light perfume, and to kiss her lips, so gently the boundaries of the magic land were not violated. Then he felt a rough hand on his shoulder that almost flung him from the bench.

Years of street fighting, of instant feline reflexes to sudden assault helped Tony bounce to his feet. His hands, formed into hard fists to throw at his target, were never launched, for he saw that Bernardo had turned away from him to look down at the girl on the bench.

He saw the destruction of their magic land. Of course, he had seen the girl come in with Bernardo. The girl in the white dress, whose name he did not even know, was Bernardo's sister. Tony was overwhelmed and terrified that he might lose the most wonderful thing he had ever found.

"Go home, American," Bernardo spat at him.

"Slow down, Bernardo," Tony said, and moved his right hand to assure the girl that everything was all right, that she could depend upon him not to fight.

Bernardo's lips twitched. "Stay away from my sister!" He turned to Maria. "Couldn't you see he was one of them?"

"No," she replied. "I saw only him, and he's done nothing wrong."

Snapping his fingers to gather the Sharks around him, Bernardo saw Chino moving rapidly across the dance floor. "I told you," he accused Maria, "there's only one thing they want from a Puerto Rican girl!"

"You're lying in your throat," Tony said.

"Cool, boy," Riff approved, as he got to Tony's side. "You tell him."

Chino tapped Bernardo's shoulder and moved past him to confront Tony. Very pale, but quiet, so that he did not look frightened, Chino measured the tall American. "Get away," he said. "Leave her alone."

"Keep out of this, Chino," Tony advised him, then turned away abruptly, fearful that Maria was going to leave.

Bernardo clamped his fingers around Maria's wrist to pull her behind him. "Now let me tell you . . ."

". . . tell me!" Riff pushed forward. "If you characters want to settle this right here outside . . ."

Murray Benowitz knew that he was shouting, but he had to get their attention. "Fellows, please! Everything was going so well. Do you fellows get pleasure out of making trouble? Come on now, it won't hurt you to have a good time." With upward gestures of his right hand, he signaled frantically for the music to start again. "Everybody dance," he suggested. "Do it for me."

Still holding his sister's wrist, Bernardo dragged her to the side of the floor which had been taken over by the Sharks. He had to jam his free hand into a pocket to keep from striking his sister.

Never before had he felt so betrayed. It was as if a knife had been planted firmly in his back by someone he trusted and loved, and for whom had she done this thing? For some goddamn Polack who had beaten up as many of her own as any American on the West Side.

"We never should have sent for you," he raged at her, still holding on to her wrist. "I warned you to stay away from them. What's the matter, you don't understand Spanish any more?"

Chino offered Maria his handkerchief which she used to dab at her eyes. "Do not yell at her, 'Nardo."

"You have to yell at babies."

"And that's what frightens them," Anita said, as she put an arm around Maria's shoulder.

"Shut up," Bernardo warned everyone. "Chino, take her home. No stopping for a soda, right home!"

Maria lowered the handkerchief. " 'Nardo, please, it's my first dance. He said nothing . . ."

"Lucky for you that you're my sister," Bernardo said angrily. "Now take her home, Chino."

There was nothing more to be said, Bernardo felt, and turned away to stride rapidly across the floor to the punch bowl, where he dipped a cup into the cold liquid and drank thirstily. He knew that things were going to come to a head and was anxious to get it over with. Sure he was upsetting his sister, but she deserved to be punished.

Nostrils flaring, Bernardo glared at the Jets and spit to show them what they were. Dirt—less than dirt. Dirt that made dirt of everything they touched, especially girls. By all the saints, they weren't going to touch a Puerto Rican girl. Not while he lived, could fight, could stab, could kill.

He could see the Jets in a tight group, and the Sharks were also ready. At the door, Chino turned to wave at him, and Bernardo nodded his head, to signal that Chino was to take Maria right home. He dipped his cup again to drink more easily, realized that his heart wasn't thumping as hard, and felt cool, man, and ready.

In a way he was glad that they were going to have the showdown tonight. Come Monday morning every Puerto Rican in the neighborhood would be able to walk with assurance. Over the rim of the cup, he saw Diesel speaking to Riff and both of them were gesturing happily as they pointed at Tony. But Bernardo wondered why the big Polack kept looking at his sister. It wasn't a dirty or disrespectful look. Too bad that Maria was going to have to learn about them, but it couldn't be helped.

He and the Sharks hadn't insulted the Americans; he and the Sharks had been willing to go along with that stupid Glad Hand and dance with the American girls. So it wasn't his fault or the fault of any of the Sharks. They wanted a showdown? Great! He wasn't the man to disappoint them.

He had got the word that the Jets were ready to challenge and that's why he had ordered the Sharks to come to the dance in full force. The Jets had shown up, which was what he wanted, and the only mistake he had made was permitting Maria to come to this dance. But it was the Americans, the Anglos, who had spoiled her good time.

Jacket closed to the third button, hands thrust into his pockets, Bernardo crossed the floor and stopped about ten feet from Riff. He knew that Pepe, Indio, and Toro were right behind him, watching carefully.

"I think you've been looking for me."

Riff nodded slowly as he looked Bernardo over from the tip of his pointed, highly polished shoes, to the tight knot in Bernardo's tie. "You heard right," Riff said. "Because we Jets want to talk to your war council—if you have one."

"The pleasure is mine," Bernardo said, and bowed stiffly from the waist. Even in discussing war, he was going to teach the Americans how gentlemen went about it.

"Let's step outside," Riff suggested.

Before Bernardo favored Riff with a cynical smile, he moved his right hand to indicate Anita, Stella, Margarita and the other girls. "My boys and I will not leave our ladies alone. Where could we meet you in—say an hour?"

"In front of the candy store in the middle of the block?" Riff suggested.

"Why not the candy store next to where I live?" Bernardo said, after a short laugh. "We will meet in front of the Coffee Pot, that's neutral territory. You know where that is? Or do you want us to drop a stink bomb so you'll find it? The American who owns it wouldn't mind."

"The Coffee Pot," Riff nodded. "And no jazz before then."

Bernardo flicked a thumb to include all the Sharks. "We know the rules—Native Boy," he spat the epithet.

"It's good to hear you know something," Riff said before he turned to Diesel. "Spread the word," he ordered.

Diesel made a circle with his thumb and forefinger. "Right, Daddy-o"—he winked at Bernardo—"I'm looking forward to introducin' my knuckles to your mouth."

"Stop jawin'," Riff ordered Diesel. "We've got to get the chicks home." He looked around and was relieved to see Tony still staring at the door. "Tony!" he called and snapped his fingers. "Over here."

Riff never knew if Tony had heard him, because the guy he considered his best friend had started to walk toward the door as if he were in a fog. There was something wrong with him, Riff concluded. He was definitely sick, mainly in the head.

But this was another secret he wasn't going to share with anyone, and to forestall any questions, he turned to speak to Action and Diesel. They were to get down to the arsenal and start moving things up, because they didn't know what Bernardo's pleasure was going to be. But whatever it was, he'd be sorry for his choice.

First things first, Tony thought, when he realized that he was on the sidewalk in front of the center.

The thing was to get away, so that Riff and the boys couldn't tie him up for the rest of the night.

Her name was Maria, a really beautiful name, one that made him think of all the most wonderful sounds possible—church bells that weren't too loud, the sweet song of a bird, the low voices of lovers, the way his mother spoke since he had gone to work. Why, even the stars in the summer sky seemed brighter.

It had happened, the thing he had been searching for, the thing that had eluded him.

All right, she was Bernardo's sister. So what? Plenty. It was bad, mighty bad, probably he could not remember anything worse. But in the movies he had seen, no matter how the family felt, the girl always felt different. And he could tell that Maria felt that way too.

He had to see her again, to make certain that she did. She was Bernardo's sister, so he knew where she lived, and then and there he would have given ten years of his life to have been able to walk up to the front door of Bernardo's flat, ring the bell and ask to see Maria Nunez.

Standing in the dark doorway of a tenement, Tony saw Riff, the Jets, and their girls pass. He heard Snowboy say they could have coffee at the Pot while they waited for Bernardo and his spics, and heard Graziella ask Riff if there was anything they could do to help.

"Plenty," Gee-Tar said. "But it'll keep until after."

"You think you'll have the strength?" Pauline scoffed.

"Enough to make you yell 'enough,'" Gee-Tar said as he copped a quick feel.

It was an effort for Tony to wait until they were around the corner. Only then did he leave the shadows and walk rapidly along the curb until he came to the tenement where Bernardo lived. He even knew the exact apartment, because six or seven months ago the Jets and he had actually considered raiding Bernardo's and working him over in the heart of his own territory.

It had been planned for him to go over the rooftops and come down the fire escape at the back of the house and kick his way through a window while Riff, Diesel, and the others shot the lock off the front door.

All the houses in the area were built pretty much alike, so the window off the fire escape was probably a bedroom, which posed a problem. Suppose her mother and father were sleeping in that bedroom?

It was a chance he would have to take, Tony thought as he ducked into the passageway that led to the backyard, and paused for a moment to orient himself.

As his eyes adjusted to the darkness, the clotheslines and occcasional pieces of wash hung in random patterns became visible. Breathing heavily, he moved a garbage can under the fire escape ladder which was beyond his reach. Climbing carefully on to the lid, he flexed his knees and leaped upward. The can tipped over but no one in the silent flats heard it. It was a sound they had grown accustomed to; dogs and cats foraged in the neighborhood and cans were always being overturned.

Rung by rung he pulled himself up the ladder until a knee touched the first crossbar, then he ascended rapidly until he reached the third story, where he began to climb slowly.

He paused at the steeply angled iron flight that led to the Nunez fire escape. He only dared go halfway up. Or should he ascend a half flight above the window? Then, if the worst happened, he would be closer to the roof. But no, he might be trapped on the roof. It would be easier to escape into the darkness below.

A telephone rang suddenly in the night. Across the yard a toilet flushed with a throaty gargle and rumbling of old pipes, a cat mewed on a back fence, a tug barge hooted mournfully from the river, a baby wailed and would not be pacified.

Tony withdrew some small coins from his pocket, prayed quickly, and threw a coin at the window. He heard the musical ping of metal against glass, then strained to hear if anyone stirred within the darkness of the room.

"Maria," he whispered. "Maria . . ."

He had to blink to believe his eyes, for there was a white figure in the window, and the figure was opening the window wider. He saw that it was Maria and took the six steps—three at a time— about to call her name, but paused because she had a finger to her lips. "Ssh," she whispered. "Quick, tell me your name."

"It's Tony." He knelt at the sill. "Anton Wyzek. It's Polish."

"It's a nice name," she whispered again. "Now you must go."

"Go? I just got here. Look, let's go somewhere where we can talk." He saw that she still wore the white dress but her hair was loose to frame her face in lovely waves. "We just gotta talk."

Maria shook her head. "You must go away."

"Do you want me to go away?"

She sat on the sill, tense and silent. "You must be very quiet."

He reached out to take her hand and place it on his heart. "What do I do about this?"

"Let it beat," she said. Suddenly she turned and looked toward the interior of the flat. "You must go. If Bernardo . . ."

"He's at the dance," Tony said, and felt guilty because he knew differently.

Maria nodded. "Soon he will have to bring Anita home."

"Does he feel about Anita like I feel about you?" he asked boldly.

"I think so," she said.

"Then he won't be coming home." Tony was proud of his logic. "Look, let's go up on the roof, just for a little while. To talk," he added, "just to talk, I swear."

"I believe you," she said to reassure him. "But if Bernardo should come home. . . . Why does he hate you?"

"Because he's got reason to." Once again, as at

the dance, he held both her hands. "That's what I want to talk to you about. Please, it's important. Unless you want me to go downstairs and come to your front door. I'll do that if you say so."

Maria leaned back to look at the skeletal outline of the fire escape and the ladder to the roof. "You'll hold me?" she asked.

"With my life," he swore.

Hand in hand they moved quietly up the fire escape. Tony whispered that Maria was not to look down, only up, at the stars, and as she climbed, he was only a half step behind her and both his arms, as they held the sides of the ladder, were a protective semicircle around her.

Step by step they climbed until Maria reached the parapet; and as she skipped over the roof covered with tar paper, she whirled again, for this was a moment to commemorate by dancing.

How strong his arms had been, how confident she had felt, how soft his voice had been in her ear as he told her not to be afraid, not to look down, only up at the stars, for the stars were looking down at them.

She ran toward him in her bare feet and grasped his hands. Silently they whirled in a circle and as her hair flew loose to brush across her face and mouth, she laughed, then paused to rest in his arms.

"Only for a minute," she said.

"Only for a minute," he repeated.

She smiled into his eyes. "A minute is not enough."

"For an hour then," he returned her smile, then was serious. "Before we make it forever."

Maria listened to the night as if it would tell her the hour. "I cannot," she said, but made no effort to free herself from his arms.

"I'm ready to stay here," he continued, "until morning. Then you can invite me downstairs for breakfast and to meet your mother and father. Do you think they'll like me?"

He felt her sadness and was sorry, but they would have to face facts and things as they were, so they could plan for the things that should be. "I like your mother, because she's your mother, your father because he's your father . . ."

"I have three younger sisters," she interrupted.

"Fine." He was enthusiastic. "I like them too. I like all your friends and relatives, and all their friends and relatives, and all their . . ."

"You did not mention 'Nardo."

Tony's sigh was deep. "I like him too, because he's your brother."

"And suppose my mother and father and my sisters and 'Nardo were not related to me? Then you would hate them?"

"Maria, you've got to hold me. The thing you've asked me is what I've been trying to keep from thinking about. Help me, Maria." He knelt to pillow his head against her slender thigh. "You've got to help me, because I'm not letting you go. I'm not," he repeated fiercely as his arms tightened about her. "I don't care who comes up here, who sees us, what anybody says or does. I'm not letting you go."

"Tony, please, stand." Her hand rested lightly on his head to stroke the short, stubby hair, which she knew would be soft and fine as silk if he let it grow. "I didn't mean to ask that."

"I'm glad you asked it." He did not want to stand but they had to look at each other, so there could be no doubt in her mind about anything he said. "I don't care if they come up here and cut my heart out," he continued. "Without you, I wouldn't want it."

"Don't say that." Her finger crossed his lips. "Without you, I do not think I would want to live either."

"Don't you know?"

"I do!" she said as her hands framed his face and she stood on tiptoe to kiss his lips. Her kiss was gentle, but as magic as Tony knew it would be. "I do," she whispered as she clung to him. "We must be together. But now you must go. Now I want to think about what we must do."

She was serious. Suddenly much older than he, feeling much wiser, she understood the primitive wilderness they inhabited. She had to return to her room and think. "It is very important that we think."

"I'll help you down the ladder. But you still must look up."

"Even if I looked down I would only see the sky," she said.

"And the stars," he added.

"And the moon. And the sun," she said.

"How could you see the sun when it's night?" His tone changed suddenly. "I'll see you tomorrow? And we'll tell each other what we thought about, and what we're going to do? Where can I see you? What time?"

"Do you know where Señora Mantanios has her bridal shop? I work there," she continued after he nodded. "I sew."

Tony held her hand against his cheek. "You be careful of the needles," he warned her. "I don't want any accidents. What time will I see you?"

"Six o'clock?"

"Six o'clock," he repeated. "What name do you like better? Tony or Anton?"

"I like them both," she said after a moment. "But Anton is more poetical. *Te adoro*, Anton," she said. "That means I love you."

He rapped his forehead to awaken his dormant and rudimentary knowledge of Polish. "Maria, *ja kocham cie*. That's Polish," he said, "and it doesn't sound as good. But it means the same thing."

"Kiss me," she said. "It's a new language for both of us. But we speak it so well." Again she looked at the stars. "Even up there"—she pointed at a bright star—"if there are a boy and girl standing on a roof, and they are able to see us, and they hear us speak, they might not understand what we say. But if they see us kiss, they will know."

"That I love you," he said, as he moved to cover her mouth with his lips.

"And that I love you," she murmured, before the wind whirled them into the sky toward the stars.

Although she had wanted to stay awake, to remember everything over and over again, sleep enveloped her in a matter of minutes, and she murmured drowsily that she was sleepy and whoever was bothering her, would they please go away?

"Wake up, Maria. It's Anita," she heard the whispering in her ear. "Wake up!"

She sat erect with a start, as a cold hand of fear fastened itself at her throat. "My God, what is the matter?"

"Nothing," Anita continued to whisper. "Bernardo wants you to come up on the roof. We are all there —Chino, Pepe, Indio. All the girls too. There is nothing the matter; we are having a party there. Suddenly you don't like parties?"

Maria yawned with relief, stretched, and ran fingers through her loose hair. "I was sleeping," she complained because she longed to return to her dreams. "And I'm not dressed."

"Nowadays it doesn't take a girl more than a minute to get dressed." Anita giggled. "Hurry, and I'll wait for you."

"Bernardo is angry?" Maria asked.

Anita pursed her lips as she raised a shoulder. "When isn't he angry? Maria, hurry, please. There are other girls who would like to be Bernardo's. Don't worry about shoes and stockings. An old pair of flats will be all right."

Chino had placed his small transistor radio on an

empty egg crate and several of the boys and girls had removed their shoes to dance in their stocking feet. But Bernardo, his elbow on a parapet, puffed hard at a cigarette, and stared with cold, dead eyes at the city all around him.

It was so large, so vast, but refused to make even a little place for him. What sort of life could he make for himself in this city? Nothing he cared for, nothing he was proud of. He would fail, but others, damn them, would suffer for his failure.

"It's about time," he replied to his sister's greeting. "I'll bet if it was that Polack, you'd have been here on the double."

"She was asleep, 'Nardo," Anita said, defending his sister. "And it seems to me you like everything on the double."

Bernardo reached out as if to pinch Anita's breast. "Since when are you complaining?" Suddenly confused, because his sister was present, Bernardo snapped his fingers. "I want to talk to you, Maria. Not like a brother, like an uncle."

Anita covered her breast by crossing her arms. "Some uncle! Lucky she has a father and a mother!"

"Who don't know this country any better than she does."

"Since when are you such an expert?" Anita challenged him.

Pepe paused in his dancing with Consuelo. "You leave it to 'Nardo," he said. "He knows the score."

"So why doesn't he write a book about America?" Anita said. "None of you is so smart. In this country girls have as much right as boys to have fun. Girls can dance with anyone they please in America."

"Really?" Bernardo bowed. "You talk as if Puerto Rico isn't part of America."

"Not for you it isn't, you immigrant," Anita flung at him. "And don't start calling me all my names because in America, I've changed it to one, and if you don't like it . . ."

Bernardo snapped his cigarette aside and wound his right hand into Anita's hair above the nape of her neck. Fingers spread, he held her so that she could not avoid his lips.

"You like?" he asked her when he ended the kiss.

Anita fluttered her eyelids. "I like."

"So behave yourself," Bernardo said, as he pushed Anita aside and beckoned to Chino. "Chino, how was my sister when you brought her home?"

Chino shuffled nervously. "All right. A little upset. But they were only dancing."

Outraged at Bernardo's behavior, Anita pushed him with both hands. "How come you're asking so many questions? As if you were a policeman or something? It's all right for a boy to be worried about his sister, but how about doing a little worrying about your girl friend and her future? You leave Maria to Chino—and her father and mother. Maybe they didn't do such a good job on their son." She stared at Bernardo, and had to smile as she admired the narrow set of his eyes, which made him look darkly romantic. "But they did all right for Maria. Look at her! And tell me you are not ashamed for thinking and speaking so ugly!"

"They don't know any more than she does," Bernardo said. "They're just babies in America—all of them."

"But she was only dancing," Anita said. "Everyone knows that."

"Only dancing," Bernardo mimicked, "with an American, who's really a Polack."

Anita pointed at Bernardo. "Look who's talking," she scoffed. "The spic . . ."

"You're not so cute," Bernardo warned.

"Since when?" Anita was not intimidated, because Bernardo's eyes told her what he was really thinking. "Because you won't ask me, I'll tell you. I think Tony is cute. And he works," she added.

Chino raised his hand for attention. "As a delivery boy." He looked at Maria, who was staring at the stars. "And you know what delivery boys become? Errand boys. And since you are going to ask me, Anita"—he bowed to her—"I'll tell you. An assistant becomes an operator. A full member of the union."

"Oh, knock it off, Chino," Bernardo interrupted angrily as he pulled a fresh cigarette from his pack and lighted it. "If that lousy Polack wants to join the union he can get in ahead of you and make more than you because he's an American."

"That isn't true," Maria interrupted her brother. It was all right to be silent, she thought, and in silence to listen and learn. But she had heard enough to know that Bernardo hated Tony, and if he continued to think and talk this way he would only hate him more.

There were many things she had to do, and one of the most important was to stop Bernardo from hating so much. Bernardo could only think of hatred and destruction and she remembered what her priest on the island had said—that those who lived by the sword would die by it.

"If Tony was born in America, he is not a Polack," she said. "Even if he were not born in America, because he wanted to come to America, he would not be a foreigner. He would be an American just like us."

Bernardo permitted the applause of Anita and the other girls to die down before he mocked his sister with a little bow. "My dear Maria, you might believe that, but he doesn't. There is only one thing that he believes. That you are easy because you are Puerto Rican!"

"That is a rotten thing to say!" Anita shouted as she put her arm around Maria. "You must apologize. Not only to Maria, but to every girl here."

"What for?" Pepe asked.

"For nothing," Anita replied flatly. "Maybe you don't know it yet, but all of us girls have learned something tonight."

"Meaning what?" Bernardo asked her.

Anita placed the heels of both palms over Maria's ears. "That because we girls came here—to America—with our hearts open, you nothings think we also came with our legs open!"

"Didn't you?" Pepe asked her.

"Pig!" Anita managed to slap him across the side

93

of the face. "You'll be sent back to Puerto Rico. Soon, I hope, and wearing handcuffs."

Pepe laughed, as he flicked at Anita's nose with his forefinger, and dodged her flailing hands. Bernardo moved Maria to one side, as the Sharks and their girls formed around Pepe and Anita, who was screaming at Pepe in Spanish.

Suddenly, the roof door opened, and Bernardo heard his name called. It was his father.

"Bernardo?" his father called again, as he tightened the belt of his bathrobe. "Maria? You were asleep."

"Didn't you hear me come in, father?" Bernardo said as he signaled for Anita and Pepe to cut it. "We were having some fun up here and I thought Maria would like to see Chino again."

"Yes, Mr. Nunez," Chino continued, "I asked Bernardo to invite Maria here. I hope you do not mind. We were just listening to the radio and talking."

"Listening and talking," Maria repeated. "Were we making too much noise, father?"

"Enough to wake me up." Mr. Nunez yawned. "But it is a nice night. Cooler. How much longer are you going to be up here, Bernardo?"

"We're leaving right now," Bernardo said. "Chino will see Maria to our door. We will take our ladies home and then all the boys will meet me at the Coffee Pot. Want to come along, father?"

"It is too late, but thank you," Mr. Nunez yawned again. "Good night." He turned to his daughter. "Maria, the door will be open."

"I will lock it, father." she said.

Again she turned to look at her brother, but his back was toward her, as he stared again into the darkness over the city.

# • CHAPTER FIVE •

The Coffee Pot was a small luncheonette with a single window, filled with bright light that gave much more illumination than was needed. But the light enabled the patroling prowl cars to see the interior, because the proprietor of the Coffee Pot was fed up with being a training establishment for cheap stick-up artists.

The menu cards on the white enameled walls were stained with a thick accumulation of grease, that obscured the identity of some of the Mexican, Puerto Rican and American dishes.

The long counter was fronted by a row of worn leathertop stools, through which some of the dirty cotton filling was visible. A tired counterman washed coffee mugs with the movements of a sleepwalker, and a sharply dressed Negro and his girl sat at the counter listening to the loud, blaring juke. When Riff turned the handle and kicked the door open, the counterman and his two customers looked up quickly. With an easy movement, the Negro slid some change across the counter, took his girl by the arm, and guided her into the street and away from trouble.

"Relax," Riff said to the frightened counterman as he held up a dollar bill. "Coffee all around. Anybody been here looking for us?"

The counterman shuffled toward the tall urn which had not been polished in years. "Nobody, Riff," he replied. "Look, fellows, just stayin' alive gives me all the trouble I can stand. So don't give me any more."

Riff snapped his fingers impatiently. "We want coffee—no cream, no sugar, no gas."

"I want sugar," Baby-John said. "I like sugar."

Ice elbowed Baby-John into the counter and the youngest member of the Jets rubbed his upper arm and slid onto a stool. Then he removed a comic book from his pocket, opened it and began to read with interest. As a junior member he had to learn to be patient and keep his mouth shut; and what he was doing now would prove to Ice that he wasn't too stupid to have got his message.

"Where the hell are they?" Ice asked as he pointed to a clock over the cash register. "If we're havin' a war council tonight they oughta be here by now."

Riff flicked his eyes toward the startled counterman who had turned toward them sharply. "You're a comedian, Ice. The coffees," he prodded the counterman. "What the hell takes you so long?"

"It's comin'," the counterman said. "I can only pour one cup at a time."

"Superman could fill all the cups so fast you couldn't even see them." Baby-John spoke like the authority he was. "You know somethin' else about Superman? He doesn't use knives. He doesn't even have to use an atomic ray gun. He leaves that for his enemies. All he uses is this." He showed a hard fist.

"You don't say?" A-Rab was interested. "He knocks down walls and everything?"

"I do so say," Baby-John replied. "He's got it all over Batman." He pointed at the door, "Hey, lock it before Mrs. Haunted House gets in."

"I heard you, stinker," Anybodys said as she slammed the door behind her. "I got as much right here as you. And I'm willin' to prove it."

"Go back there and sit down," Riff ordered. He was too busy tonight to run her ass out on the sidewalk. "Give her some coffee," he told the counterman.

"Sure, sure," the counterman said, and looked nervously toward the street. Damn the cops, they were never around at the right time. "I'm closin' up soon."

Gee-Tar shook his head. "It's against the law to throw out cash customers. What's the matter, bud, you don't like our manners? Now finish serving those coffees and get back to your sink until we call you."

"I'm not lookin' for trouble," the counterman pleaded, "so why pick on me?"

"We're not pickin' on anybody," Riff said as he looked at the clock again. He had been unable to find Tony, and Action had said nothing, just looked, which was worse. "Meetin' here was Bernardo's idea. You know Bernardo?"

"Sort of," the counterman said.

"He doesn't care who he knows," Anybodys called out.

Riff gestured for her to remain quiet. "Give her a doughnut or somethin'," he said to the counterman. "How come you look so starved? Don't you ever go home?"

"The answer to that is no," she said.

Baby-John looked up from his comic book, annoyed that Anybodys had been reading the balloon dialogue aloud. "Then you should be out walkin' the streets like your sister."

Anybodys' knuckles cracked Baby-John across the side of the head. "Go ahead," she challenged, "tell Superman I clobbered you one and I'll do the same to him."

The counterman had served the last mug of coffee, placed a doughnut on a paper napkin, and pushed it toward Anybodys. "I need another sixty cents," he said. "And I'm forgettin' about the tax."

"Keep the change, my good man," Mouthpiece said, as he crumpled a dollar bill and threw it at the counterman.

"I haven't seen Bernardo all night," the counterman said. "If you ask me, he's not goin' to show.

As a matter of fact, he hardly ever comes in here, seein' as he owes the boss five bucks."

"He'll be here," Riff said, as he blew across the rim of the mug. "He chose this neutral territory for our board meeting. We're gonna debate with the PR's about their place in society. Want to join us?"

"Sorry, I've got previous plans to get drunk, get picked up, and get sent to the work house for thirty days," the counterman replied. "So, no insult intended, but I'm gonna have to turn down your invitation. But why don't you take some advice? Go home and forget it."

"We can't hear you," Diesel said as he cupped his ears with both hands. "What kind of weapons do you think he's gonna choose?"

"Ask Bernardo," Riff said, as he left his stool to open the door, "because here he comes."

Baby-John put away the comic book and Anybodys whirled her stool around, so that she could rest her dirty elbows on the counter behind her. With exaggerated courtesy, Riff opened the door wide and gestured for Bernardo and the Sharks to enter.

Bernardo looked around, was convinced that no ambush was possible, and the movement of his shoulder told the Sharks to follow him into the small restaurant.

"Hope we didn't keep you waiting," Bernardo broke the silence.

"We enjoyed it," Riff replied. "How about some coffee?"

"Let's get down to business."

Riff looked at the clock, then at Action. "Bernardo hasn't learned the procedures of gracious livin'."

"Bullshit," Bernardo said, "I don't like you either." He turned to the counterman. "Cut some of these lights and get busy in the back room."

"Now I don't want no trouble in here," the counterman protested.

In exasperation, and to prove that he was as tough as Bernardo, Riff moved around the counter to flick the light switch before he pushed the counterman toward the back. "You've been workin' too hard. Relax. We're not gonna break up the joint. But we don't want you giving us no trouble. And stay away from that phone!"

"The pay phone's out front," the counterman said. "Do me a favor. Keep your word about no trouble in here."

Riff refused to be bothered with an answer as he returned to double-lock the front door and look again out into the street. Tony wasn't around. Suppose Bernardo wanted to get rolling tonight? He would have to go along.

"Bernardo, we're challenging you. All out, and once and for all."

"We accept," Bernardo said, and waited until the chorus of assent was still. "On what terms?"

"Whatever terms you're callin' for." Riff spread his hands. "We've decided to let you call it."

"You started it," Pepe said.

"Because of you, we're finishing it," Riff said to Pepe and Nibbles. "You're a couple of pretty low-down punks to jump a kid in the movies. And we're not forgettin' what you did to him—toilet and all."

Bernardo had to smile. "A bath—any kind—could only do him some good. Anyway who jumped me the first day I moved here?"

"Who asked you to move here?"

"My mother and father," Bernardo replied. "Can you say the same?"

"You dirty spic bastard, I'm gonna teach you some manners," Action said as he rose from the counter.

Bernardo spread his feet in a fighting stance. "I'm waiting, you mick sonofabitch. But I don't think you're much of a teacher."

"Hold it." Riff got between them. "Do you or don't you accept?"

"We accept," Bernardo said. "Name the time."

"You name it," Riff said.

Bernardo thought for a moment. "Tomorrow night?"

"Fine!" Riff was delighted; now he could find Tony. To seal the commitment and show the Jets how a real leader behaved, he offered Bernardo his hand. "Where's it gonna be? The park or the river?"

"How about under the highway?" Bernardo suggested as he shook Riff's hand.

Riff nodded that the battlefield was acceptable to him. "What about the weapons?"

"Suit yourself."

About to elaborate to prove that the Sharks were ready for anything the Jets could heave, swing, or throw at them, Bernardo saw someone outside the door of the luncheonette and recognized the lousy Polack who had been dancing with his sister. He moved to open the luncheonette door and admit Tony. "Your big man is here," he challenged Riff and knew that he had scored. "Maybe you want us to repeat everything?"

Tony looked through the luncheonette window at the blinking traffic signal a block away. It was red now, as if to warn him of danger and that he must react slowly. At the end of the block the broken letters of a neon sign sputtered fitfully, and the silence of the street was broken by a sharp burst of laughter from a passing car.

"You don't have to repeat nothing," Tony said. "All I'm interested in is what's this gonna be with?"

"Maybe knives and guns," Riff said, because he wanted to impress Tony with his guts.

"I thought so," Tony replied. "Just what I'd expect from a coop full of chickens."

"Who're you callin' chicken?" Action pushed forward to line up his chin with Tony's. "I'm listening."

"Every dog knows his own," Bernardo stood up to the Polack. "So I guess you weren't talking to us."

Earlier that night Tony had hidden from the Jets. Now, for reasons which he knew they could not understand, he had sought them out. But he had done so as much for Bernardo as for his sister. If it was at all possible, he had to prove to Bernardo that he had a right to see Maria, that he had left the Jets because he no longer cared to war on the

Sharks, that he was grown up, a man who understood what being in love meant.

"I'm calling all of you chicken," he said at last. "How come you have to use bricks, or knives or guns? What's the matter, afraid to get in close and slug it out?" He showed them his white, hard knuckles. "Afraid to use plain skin?"

"What kind of rumble is plain skin?" Baby-John demanded. "At least you gotta use garbage."

"We gave them the choice of weapons," Riff explained to Tony. "We're gonna use our fists anyway, so it's up to them."

"Both of you are ducking," Tony continued. He had to talk quickly while he held the psychological advantage. "A fair fight can settle anything. That's if you've got the guts to risk it. And if each side's got a good man willing to slug it out."

"I'd enjoy that," Bernardo said quickly, his eyes indicating that he hoped Tony would represent the Jets. "Let it be a fair fight."

" 'Nardo," Pepe called in dismay, "you mean the rest of us just get to look?"

"I'm not standing around for anyone!" Action said, as he smashed his empty coffee mug on the counter. "Not this man!"

"The commanders say yes or no," Riff told Action, then turned to Bernardo. "Okay, fair fight it is. We shake on it?"

"We don't have to shake again," Bernardo said. "You've got my word for it, and why wait until tomorrow night when we can go right now?" He paused to look at Tony. "I'll be waiting for you under the highway."

"Correction," Riff said, as he beckoned for Diesel to step forward. "This is our best fist man. And tomorrow night suits us fine."

Unable to hide his disappointment, Bernardo pointed at Tony. "But I thought . . ."

"Who're you choosin'?" Riff asked.

"Me," Bernardo said as he looked at Tony and decided that Maria would have to be married to Chino sooner than they had planned. "I'm representing the Sharks."

Diesel clasped both hands above his head. "The honor overwhelms me."

"I offered to shake on it," Riff said to Bernardo. "Because you didn't shake, does that mean you're backing out?"

Action thrust himself forward to gain the attention of the Sharks. "Look, Bernardo," he began, "if you wanna change your mind, this is one man who is willin' to listen."

"Shut up, Action," Riff said quickly. "We've got a gentleman caller. Get the door open."

Detective Schrank eased himself into the luncheonette as the counterman returned from the back room and looked unhappily from the boys to the detective. "Good evening, Detective Schrank. I was closin' up as soon as the boys got finished."

Schrank leaned across the counter to take an almost full pack of cigarettes from the counterman's shirt pocket. "Mind?"

"Why should I?" the counterman said. "It's been that way all my life."

Schrank slowly lit the cigarette, took several hard puffs, and flicked the burned-out match into the nearest mug of coffee, which was Tiger's. "I always make it a rule to smoke in the can," he began slowly. "But what else is a room with half-breeds in it, eh, Riff?"

He paused and saw that Bernardo's move toward him had been checked by Riff, and this gesture proved what Glad Hand had told him—the boys were going to rumble and this was a war council.

"Clear out, spics," he said pleasantly to Bernardo. "Sure, it's a free country and I ain't got the right to order you out of here. But I've got a badge and until you take it to court, you do like I say." He pointed at the door with his cigarette. "Beat it. And that means off the street."

Schrank watched the Sharks file out in cold silence and gather around Bernardo. Before Krupke could get out of the prowl car the Sharks split up and scattered in all directions. It was impossible to follow them and Schrank gestured to Krupke to remain in the driver's seat.

"Well, Riff, where's the rumble gonna be?" He paused for a reply, nodded at several of the boys and saw how they turned away. When he took a step toward Baby-John and Anybodys, both became busy with an adventure in the comic book. "Ah, look, I know regular Americans don't get together with the gold teeth unless they're gonna rumble. The river? The park?"

When he continued his voice was tighter, with more bite in it. "I'm for *you*," he said. "I want this beat cleaned up. So do you. So why don't we help each other? Where're ya gonna rumble? The playground? Sweeney's lot?"

He mentioned another battlefield, and waited for some response. "Dirty little hoodlums," he exploded in rage, "I oughta drag ya down to the station house and have your skulls mashed to pulp! You and the tin-horn immigrant scum you come from! How's your old man's d.t.'s, A-Rab? How's the action on your mother's mattress, Action?"

Schrank moved lightly on the balls of his feet, as his right hand went for the blackjack. Ready now, he waited for Action to leap toward him, but Riff and Gee-Tar had moved to pin the raging boy between them.

"Let'm go, buddy-boy, just let'm go," Schrank suggested. "Because one of these days, there won't be nobody to hold him." Keeping his eyes on the boys, his hand on the blackjack, Schrank retreated toward the door. "I'll find out where you're gonna rumble," he promised them. "But he sure to finish each other off before I get there. Because if you don't, I will."

The Jets waited until the prowl car drove off before they left the luncheonette. At the door, Riff waited for Tony but his friend sat at the dirty counter and brooded over his taut, clasped hands.

"Comin' along, Tony?" Riff asked.

Tony sat for a moment, then swung slowly around

on the stool. "Why didn't you match me against Bernardo?"

"Because Diesel don't mind fightin' dirty. And you, Tony, I don't know about you anymore. Another thing . . ."

"Yes?"

"If it's man-to-man, Diesel's expendable. And you'n me know Bernardo. That joker is someone I don't trust." Riff paused to grimace at his right hand before he wiped the palm along his trouser leg. "Can you imagine me shaking hands with one of them, especially him?"

"I can imagine it."

Riff controlled his temper. "Another thing, Tony, you're my friend and the last guy I wanna see hurt. But if Diesel gets beat, we can still call on you. How about that?"

"Drop dead."

"Anything for a friend. Say"—Riff cocked his head—"how's that sister of Bernardo's? Think you're gonna make out? Boy, wouldn't that be giving it to Bernardo?" He made an obscene gesture with his right arm.

"Know what I've got to say to you?" Tony asked. "Bernardo and you—both together? Hell's too good for you."

"What's eatin' you, Mac?" Riff blustered. "Does that mean you're writing us off?"

Tony rose from the stool. "It means anything you want it to mean." His voice trembled. "Now get the hell outa here before I do Schrank a favor and work you over."

# · CHAPTER SIX ·

"Are you all right, Anton?" Mrs. Wyzek called from her chair at the kitchen window.

Leaning into the kitchen from the bathroom where he was shaving, traces of soap still on his chin and around both ears, Tony winked at his mother. "Sure I'm all right, Ma," he said. "Except you shouldn't yell that way when I'm shaving." He held up the safety razor. "This thing's sharp."

"I'm sorry," his mother said as she moved her feet in the pan of cold water. "It's so hot and you had to work all day."

"I didn't mind," Tony said. "And it keeps me from getting fat."

Mrs. Wyzek looked at her son and smiled. For so long and sorry a time he had been a stranger and now he was her son again. How and why the change had taken place she dared not ask; but tomorrow, as every Sunday for the last five, almost six months, she would recite prayers of thanksgiving for the change in Anton.

If only his father had been alive to see the change. But he had died very young, at Tarawa, when Anton had been no more than an infant, and had not shared her bewilderment, terror and confusion at not understanding why he and all the other boys in this awful neighborhood had to become bums and gangsters.

Then the change had come and Anton had become the son she had hoped for after her marriage, the son she had known as a little boy, the son she had prayed for as she had stained her pillow with bitter tears, because he had become a dangerous stranger for whom she maintained a home he returned to only when he tired of the streets. Whatever it was—her prayers or something else that had happened to Anton—she was thankful, grateful, every moment of the day and night.

Mrs. Wyzek looked at the little fan that Anton had placed on the gas range and nodded her approval of the hum of its motor and the cool little breeze it blew across half the kitchen. Between the fan and her feet in a pan of cold water, she was very comfortable and happy. "You'll have a cold drink with me before you go out tonight?" she asked.

"Sure, Ma. Soon as I get dressed. What time is it?"

"Almost eight-thirty," She raised her right hand to hold it in the cool gust of air blown by the fan. "I'm so comfortable."

"Good," Tony winked. "Now you mind if I finish shaving?"

"No, Anton," his mother said. "Be careful. Don't cut yourself."

The mirror had become fogged with the heat of the room and Tony wiped the glass clean with the side of a hand before he leaned forward and screwed up the corner of his mouth to get at a difficult place which he often missed. As he ran the lukewarm water over the blade, he frowned at himself in the mirror, leaned both hands on the edge of the little bathroom sink, and wondered—just exactly how were things going to go tonight? So far, the question stumped him, and he thought again of his meeting with Maria.

His lips formed her name, he approved their shape. Maria was a good name to identify with the sun, the moon, stars and love.

Try as hard as he could, it had been more difficult to think of Maria than of the Jets and the Sharks. About three that afternoon Baby-John had come into the drugstore to buy a new comic book, and whispered that he was speaking for all the boys, and they were sure glad to see him back with the Jets; even if he hadn't been chosen by Riff to take on Bernardo. The Jets knew they could count on him, and Riff wanted Tony to meet them under the highway by nine o'clock.

"I just stole me a new icepick from the five and ten," Baby-John had said proudly. "And I made me a sheath and I'm gonna wear it down the back of my neck. So if them lousy Sharks don't go along with Diesel licking their man, we'll just take them on. And I'm personally gonna give it to Pepe and Nibbles." He touched the scab on his earlobe. "I'm gonna push it right through so they can wear earrings just like their broads."

He had given Baby-John a free cold bottle of soda, and told him not to show that night. But he knew that Baby-John wouldn't listen; instead he would hurry to tell the other Jets what he had said. Some of them, especially Action, and Diesel too, would say that he had really turned yellow and wouldn't be there. Riff would have a bad time of it, so like it or not, for Riff's sake, he had to show.

At five o'clock he had drawn his pay, fifty dollars for fifty hours, bought an electric fan wholesale, run home with it and taken a quick bath, because cleaning up in the cellar of the drugstore was impractical. He'd told his mother that he wasn't hungry, that it was too hot to eat, and he would be back later.

At five-thirty he had concealed himself behind the door of a tenement across the street from the bridal shop until he had seen the woman who ran the shop leave, and minutes before six he saw Bernardo's well-stacked chick come out. He had cursed when Anita had returned to knock at the door, which Maria had opened, but Anita had, at last, gone on.

Now, his heart pounding so loud the drumming filled his ears, Tony ran all the way to the back door of the store.

Yes, it was the same girl that had flown with him on the wind the night before, and in silence she offered him her hand he followed her into the shop.

"I thought it would never get to be six."

"I too was watching the clock," Maria said. "The minute hand did not move."

"That's how it seemed to me too." He paused to look around the store. "It isn't so hot in here."

"That's what the Señora said. She said it was cooler here than in her flat. I thought she would never go home."

Tony fingered a scrap of white silk. "But she did. Then I saw that other girl come back."

"Anita?"

"I guess that's her name," he said. "Bernardo's girl."

"Yes, Anita. She wanted me to go home with her." Maria flung her arms wide in imitation of Anita. "You know what she calls the Señora?"

"Old bag?"

"That and something else. A *bruja*."

"What's that?"

Maria giggled. "A witch."

"That's not so bad," Tony said. "But I don't think there's a broom strong enough to carry her."

Maria giggled. "I must tell that to Anita. She wanted me to go home with her so she could give me some"—she thought for a moment—"bubble-bath?"

"Today Doc sold a lot of that in the drugstore. I should've brought you a present. What kind does Anita use?"

"Black Orchid."

Tony shook his head because the name did not suit her. "We've got better than that in stock," he said. "Tomorrow I'm gonna bring you some. And some other things too."

"You mustn't, Anton."

"Why not, Maria?"

She turned to study a pattern laid out on the cutting table. "Anita is going home to make herself pretty and exciting."

"So?"

Maria turned toward him, her mouth turned down at the corners. "For Bernardo, after the rumble. Why do they have to fight, I asked her? And do you know what she said? She said that the boys fight for the excitement which becomes so big that dancing and"—she paused and blushed—"even girls are not enough excitement for the feeling. Anita says that after a fight my brother is so healthy, that she really does not have to use the Black Orchid." She paused. "Anita knows you are coming here. It was the only way to make her go away."

"I see," Tony was solemn. "And what did she say?"

"That you and me—we are both crazy. Out of our heads."

"Then she doesn't like my seeing you any more than Bernardo does?"

Maria shook her head and her eyes told Tony that even if this had been Anita's opinion, she would not have honored it. "She said that we must be out of our heads to think we could see each other. She said it was impossible."

"See how wrong she is?" Tony asked.

"She is on our side," Maria said. "But she is also worried for us."

"We're untouchable, Maria. You and me. And I'm gonna tell you why." He rested his hands, suddenly clammy, lightly on her shoulders and moved his head until his eyes looked directly into hers. "Because we're still on a cloud. And that kind of magic doesn't go away."

"Magic is also black and evil." She shuddered. "Anton—Tony, I must know. You will tell me the truth?"

"Now and forever."

"You are going to that rumble?"

He exhaled, then shook his head. "Until you asked me, I didn't know for sure. I was mixed up about it. Now I'm not. The answer is, no. The only thing I'm doing tonight is go home, get dressed, and call for you."

"Before you come to see me I must speak to my mother and father." She was firm. "And before I do that you must stop the fight."

"I did stop it," he insisted. "Last night. It's not going to be anything except a fist fight. And Bernardo can't really get hurt."

"No." She continued to shake her head. "No fight is good for us."

"Maria, I've been here longer than you. I mean . . ." He paused, confused, for he had seen how she shuddered. "I mean that the fight has nothing to do with us. Nothing will happen," he insisted. "Nothing. And smile again. Please."

"Only if you do this for me," she said. "It is not for me, but for us that I ask. You must stop it."

"You asked for us," he said. "So I will."

"Can you?" She thanked him by squeezing his hands. "You can?"

"You don't want even a fist fight? There won't be any. You name it and I deliver," he bragged.

"I believe you." She clapped her hands with awe. "You have magic."

It was the time to embrace her, to hold her in his arms again, and she rested, as if wearied by the heat, with her head on his shoulder. "Could you wear the white dress again? You see, I didn't really get a chance to get a good look at it."

"The white dress?"

"The white dress." His lips brushed the outline of her ear as he murmured her name. "For tonight when I come by for you."

"You cannot come for me!" She was frightened. "My momma . . ."

". . . is going to meet mine," he interrupted. "But first I gotta meet your mother. So I can invite her along when I take you to meet mine. You see, Maria, I have one too. My father, he's been dead a long time."

"I'm so sorry, Anton." Maria moved to free herself and Tony released her reluctantly. "I don't know," she hesitated.

"But I do." He was confident. "Now watch closely," he said as he brushed at his arms as if he were rolling up both sleeves. "Nothing up either of them. And you said I have magic? So—" He pointed at a nearby dress dummy which had been drapped with a pale yellow scarf. He waggled his fingers at the dummy, then turned to Maria. "My mother. See, she's coming from the kitchen to say hello. That's where she is most of the time when she's home. In the kitchen."

"She is dressed so elegant for the kitchen," Maria whispered as if in awe.

"Because I told her you were coming in your white dress." Standing behind the dummy, Tony moved the figure from side to side. "See, she's looking you over. Sort of saying to herself . . . that you're sort of pretty. A little skinny, but if Tony likes you that way, she does too."

Maria's hands outlined a heavy woman. "She is . . . ?"

"She doesn't mind if you say she's sort of . . . well built. Just never say she's fat."

"I will not say it," Maria said as she skipped over to another dress dummy of slenderer proportions. "This is my momma." She peeked around the dummy to laugh at Tony. "And I take after her."

"Hello, Mrs. Nunez, My boy Tony has told me all about your daughter. And I must say she's as nice as he says she is."

"Thank you, Mrs. Wyzek." Entered into the spirit of the delightful game, Maria moved her dummy from side to side. "This is my husband, Mr. Nunez."

"How do you do, Mrs. Wyzek?"

"How do you do, Mr. Nunez? I want to talk to you about my son. You see, he's really gone—I mean, in love with your daughter. And he would like to talk to you about Maria."

"First we will talk about Tony," Maria said. "Does he go to church?"

"He used to. And he will start again." Tony came from behind the dummy and knelt before it. "May I have your daughter's hand?"

Maria came slowly out from behind the dummy, for a moment stared anxiously, then clapped her hands. "He says yes! My momma too! Now you ask your mother."

"I already have." He reached for Maria's hand and kissed her fingers. "Right now she's kissing your cheek."

"They will want a church wedding."

"So will my mother," Tony said. Ruefully, he scratched his head. "I'm gonna have a lot of explaining to do to the father. But when he meets you, he'll see—"

"Anton . . ."

"And what I'll say to you about loving and honoring and holding you until I die, I'll mean every word of it. So help me, Maria. And it'll be the easiest thing I've ever had to swear to."

"I love you, Tony. And I want only that you will be happy."

"We'll both be happy," he insisted. "That's the way it's gonna be. I swear."

"Then I swear too." She kissed him again, even more gently, and stepped back to look at him with smiling eyes and lips. "I'll wear the white dress," she said. "And I will be waiting for you to come to my house after you stop the fight."

"It's a breeze," Tony said. He looked at the clock on the wall with surprise. "It's almost seven. Your mother and father will be worried. Let me walk you home."

"No, you must go out the back way," she insisted. "I will lock the store and draw the shutter. Tony, what should I tell my mother and father—I mean about my wearing the white dress?"

"That you're going out with a boy who's gonna call for you," he explained patiently. "And when I get there, they'll see that it's me."

He had felt so good that he just had to walk and smile at the world so that almost another hour was wasted. Then, when he got home, his mother insisted that he at least drink something cold. Only after he finished the glass of milk in two gulps was he able to escape into the bathroom. "Ma," he called as he rinsed the razor for the last time, "what time is it?"

"Almost a quarter of nine, Anton."

"I've gotta hurry," he said, as he ran from the bathroom into his bedroom.

"You're wearing your new suit?"

"Natch."

"It looks nice on you," she said. "It's nice to see you getting dressed up. But I wish you'd stop for a real shoe shine."

"I'll do that," he called, as he slipped a tie under his shirt collar, then decided to put it in his coat pocket and put it on just before he got to Maria's.

Maybe, if things worked out, he would be able to tell Bernardo exactly how things were, and if he wouldn't listen, then someone was going to have to knock some sense into him, which would be his job, not Diesel's. Hurry, he told his reflection in the mirror, the sooner you get to the highway, the sooner you get to Maria's.

Riff tossed aside his beer can, wiped his lips, and looked again at his watch. It was ten to nine and time to get started.

"All right," he instructed the tense, nervous Jets, "we'll scatter and move over to the highway. And for chrissakes, watch out for Schrank. He's been on my tail all day."

The Jets melted into the darkness. In the next street Bernardo gave similar orders to the Sharks.

"You gonna have to make it home tonight?" he asked Anita.

She pressed herself to him and rotated her hips slowly. "I told my mother I was staying with Maria. She said okay. But just where are we gonna go?"

"We'll see," he said. "I gotta run."

"Take care of yourself, 'Nardo. And hurry. I'll be waiting right here."

Bernardo waved again, and moved off down the street. A block away he paused in the hallway to check the spring on his switchblade knife. The hard instant click as the blade sprang out and locked into position gave him a feeling of confidence. With this knife he was going to stab deep into an alien world.

119

For the knife made him as big as anyone, bigger, because it could cut anyone down to his size, cut someone into little pieces he could kick aside. Bernardo put the knife away.

He wasn't planning to use it tonight, but if the Jets thought he wasn't ready to play it cool, if they started something funny, they were going to be in for a sharp surprise. Seven inches of surprise.

Bernardo waited for a car to pass him, then darted across the road and dug his heels into the embankment as he descended slowly, with care, because this was no time to turn an ankle. His eyes were accustomed to the dark and he could see that despite the heat some of the Sharks wore their jackets over T shirts.

With a sharp signal he identified himself, heard Chino and Pepe call his name, and heard one of the Jets say that the chief spic had finally shown. Spic . . . sometime when he had the time he would show them what a spic could really do. Man, the blood would really flow.

"Fan out," he ordered the Sharks. "And keep your eyes on me. If they start anything . . ."

"We'll be watching, 'Nardo," Toro said. "We don't trust them no how."

"I'll second you," Chino said as Bernardo began to remove his shirt.

"Fine," Bernardo agreed. He flexed the muscles of his back and shoulders, and checked the knife in his pocket. "Let's go."

"Our man is ready." Chino called.

"So's ours," Riff said. "Let'm come center and shake hands."

Bernardo spit into the darkness. "For what?"

"Because that's how it's done," Riff said, after he turned to laugh with the Jets at the ignorant PR's.

"More gracious living?" Bernardo asked. "Look . . ." He pointed at Diesel and Riff, but included all the Jets and anyone like them. "I don't go for that pretend crap you go for in this country. "Every one of you hates every one of us . . ."

"You're so right," Riff interrupted.

". . . and we hate you double, right back. I don't drink with nobody I hate." Bernardo spat again, "So I don't shake hands with nobody I hate." Fists raised and ready, he stepped forward carefully.

"Okay," Riff said, "if that's that way you want it." He stepped to one side and signaled Diesel. "He's all yours."

Scowling heavily as he opened and shut his right fist, Diesel moved in slowly. He was heavier than Bernardo and the light wasn't as good as he would have liked it; but he was confident of being able to take anything Bernardo threw. Still, he was careful, for although the spic was light he had a reputation as a hard hitter. Bernardo had built up a real rep as a street fighter and there were some who said that if he could get the hate out of his system, really be cool and businesslike about it, he could at the very least become a good TV welterweight, because he could hit like a light-heavy.

Diesel threw a tentative jab with his left which the spic avoided by taking a backward step before he countered with his own left and Diesel brushed it aside easily. Again Diesel threw the left, feinted as if to throw the right and moved his head in time to avoid Bernardo's fist, which just grazed his ear.

The spic was going to try for a knockout, which meant he wasn't going to work the body, and this suited Diesel just fine because Bernardo would be working with his hands high. If he managed to land a hard one in Bernardo's gut, the spic would double like a pretzel, and a hook would straighten and set him up for a hard smash to the mouth that would loosen at least three or four of those nice white teeth.

Taking Bernardo's short left on the shoulder, Diesel countered with his own left to Bernardo's ribs. The punch lost its power because Bernardo had rolled with it, but not before his own left flicked Diesel's lip, which began to swell.

The American was tough, Bernardo knew, and as his hand grazed Diesel's mouth, he wanted to crow with triumph. His feet certain and confident, Bernardo moved around Diesel, darting in to land one, take one, and skip away and start again.

Fighting was like dancing; it had certain steps and rhythms, and once they were learned they were executed naturally, without really thinking about them. He would circle clockwise just a little longer, jabbing and hooking, feinting and ducking, then begin to circle counter-clockwise. This might throw Diesel and make him drop his hands for a second, which was all Bernardo needed for the one clean shot.

Bernardo heard someone call and stumbled awkwardly to one side. then saw that Diesel had also stepped backward. "Just hold it!"

"It's Tony," someone called. "Better late than never."

Tony breathed heavily as he stood between them.

"What's with you?" Riff said, stepping forward.

"All of you, hold your water," Tony said as he moved to keep Bernardo and Diesel from throwing punches at each other.

"Man, you're in deep water," Riff said angrily. "Just what the hell are you doing? You better talk fast, Tony."

Resting easily, breathing through parted lips, Bernardo corkscrewed the knuckles of his right fist into his left palm. "Maybe he has found the guts to fight his own battles." he observed, and smiled as the Sharks laughed at his joke.

Tony also laughed and the smile stayed on his lips as he offered Bernardo his hand. "It doesn't take guts if you have a battle, 'Nardo. But we haven't got one."

Bernardo slapped the side of Tony's hand before he gave him a hard push and sent him sprawling into the dirt. "To you and all other trash, the name is Bernardo, and after tonight it's gonna be Mr. Bernardo."

"That's enough," Riff said, as he helped Tony to his feet and gestured for the Jets to relax, that he had the situation covered. "The deal is a fair fight between you and Diesel."

Bernardo moved in and hit Tony a light backhand slap across the face. "Don't be impatient, you'll get yours later," he warned Diesel. "First I'm gonna take on pretty-boy for a warm-up." He taunted Tony, who was rubbing his cheek. "What's the matter, pretty-boy? You afraid? Chicken? Gutless?"

Riff pushed Tony behind him. "Cut it," he warned Bernardo.

But Tony refused to line up with the Jets. He could see now how serious an error he had made.

It would have been better—no matter what he told or promised Maria—to have let them have it out. If Diesel had taken Bernardo, everything would have been settled, and he could then have made a real grandstand play by offering to take on Diesel to prove to Bernardo that he wanted peace between them.

If 'Nardo had taken Diesel, he could have offered to shake hands with his future brother-in-law, and if 'Nardo had refused, and pushed him around, tried for a clean shot at Bernardo. Then when he came to, he could have offered to shake hands or put him away again.

It was too late to do any of these things now, and Tony trembled as he felt Bernardo's cold hatred. There was nothing he could do now. It was too late. But for Maria, he had to try; he was even willing to crawl.

"Bernardo, you've got it wrong." Tony kept his voice low and steady.

Bernardo shook his head. "I've got it right. You're chicken."

"Why won't you understand?" Tony asked, as he signaled for Action to keep his mouth shut.

Bernardo stepped in, one hand cupped at his ear, as the other flicked Tony's nose. "Can't hear you, chicken," he taunted Tony. "What did you say? A-Rab wants you to get me. But you're too chicken."

"Bernardo—*don't.*"

Delighted with himself, Bernardo danced around Tony to flick at his nose, his chin, to slap him across an ear, to pirouette like a bullfighter. "I can't call him *toro* because he's a chicken," he told the delighted Sharks. "Come on, chicken," he continued to taunt Tony. "What have you got to say before I start making you lay eggs?"

It was too much for Riff to take. He thought with shame of all the times, the days and weeks and months, he had spent in defending Tony, his best friend, against Action and Diesel, even against Baby-John and Anybodys. It didn't make sense. No white man who had any pride would take what this spic was dishing out. Was Tony sick in the head or something to take crap from a goddamn spic? Maybe Tony didn't feel ashamed, because someone who was sick, or without guts, couldn't, but he did. He touched his hip pocket and felt the reassuring bulk of his switchblade knife.

Bernardo slapped Tony again. "Yellow-bellied chicken . . ."

"For chrissake, Tony!" Riff shouted in anguish.

"You crazy son of a bitch, are you crazy! Don't let him do that!"

"Murder him, Tony!" Anybodys screeched.

Baby-John hopped up and down. "Kill him!"

"Kill nobody," Bernardo mocked. "You dirty, lousy . . ."

With a cry of rage, Riff pushed Tony aside and leaped for Bernardo's throat. He knocked him off balance, reached down, yanked him to his feet, and pounded his fist squarely into Bernardo's mouth.

Bernardo felt his mouth fill with blood, but lowered his head to butt Riff squarely in the face, and as Riff lost his grip and stumbled backward, Bernardo had his knife out. As he wiped his mouth, he saw the glint of Riff's blade. This was it, the way it should be. He ordered the Sharks to stay back, that was what he wanted. From the corner of his eye, he saw Tony start forward but Action and Diesel grabbed him.

Jockeying for position, feinting, moving the knives in defensive circles, both leaders decreased the distance between them. Each had had enough experience to know that this kind of fight never lasted long. It might be over with one thrust; it never took more than two or three.

Around them the perimeter constricted, and as Diesel and Action moved forward they loosened their hold on Tony for a moment, which was enough time for him to break free.

The action was a blur. He heard Riff shout at him to get back, goddamnit, and as Riff gestured to make the command more emphatic, he swept his left arm wide. It provided the few seconds Bernardo needed to come in fast and swing the knife upward in a hard lethal arc that ended in Riff's ribcage, just under the heart.

Riff was dead before he fell, and with a cry of anguish, Tony scooped the knife from his limp hand and charged forward with such sudden speed that Bernardo was caught unprepared. Unable to shift his feet properly to defend himself, all ten inches of the blade pierced his side, and dying, he fell to the ground.

The rattle and gasp of death, the darkening earth, the limp forms so suddenly cut off from hatred, violence and life, seemed too awful to endure. Then the howl of a siren, a police prowl car screaming to a stop above them, a searchlight beam probing the side of the highway, scattered the Jets and Sharks.

Diesel grabbbed Tony's arm and as Tony ran, his eyes blinded by tears, his world going up in flames, he called her name again and again and again, but only the wild despairing sound of the siren answered him.

# • *CHAPTER SEVEN* •

The transistor radio was tuned to a station that prided itself on playing only fast, driving records, with a simple primitive beat and senseless lyrics. The girls on the roof moved their feet and their shoulders, as they stared impatiently off into the darkness. Why, it was nine-thirty already, and this could only mean real live strong action. Oh, they were impatient—the loving was going to be furious tonight.

Consuelo looked at herself in a pocket mirror and decided she preferred her left profile—longer false lashes, and larger falsies. "This is my last night as a blonde," she announced.

"That's no loss," Rosalia said.

"A gain!" Consuelo returned the mirror to her large purse. "The fortune teller told Pepe a dark lady was coming into his life."

"So that's why he's not taking you out after the rumble!" Delighted with her wit, Rosalia crossed the roof to tell Maria in detail how she had just told off Consuelo, who was even more stupid than she admitted to.

The criss-crossing sounds of racing sirens in the streets below made Maria shudder. There were certain sounds she disliked, hated, even feared, and the sound of sirens inspired in her all three reactions. Sirens almost always meant trouble—illness, an accident, death, fire. Still these sirens had nothing to do with her.

"There is not going to be a rumble," she said to Rosalia.

Rosalia pointed at her. "Another fortune teller!"

Maria looked over the ledge at the street below and wondered how much longer she would have to wait for Tony. Not that there was any need for him to hurry for her mother and father had gone to the movies with her younger sisters.

She had begun to quarrel with her younger sisters when her father, to end the quarrel, had suggested they all go to the movies. The little girls were sure to fall asleep and as long as they were in the theater, they would certainly be more comfortable than at home.

She had sponsored this suggestion with enthusiasm, but told her mother and father she would stay at home because she would be going out with Bernardo and Anita and some of the other girls who were coming over.

"Where is Chino escorting you after the rumble that is not going to be a rumble?" Maria heard Consuelo ask.

Maria turned toward her to smile enigmatically. "Chino is escorting me no place."

"She is just dolling up for us." Rosalia said, as she pointed to Maria in her white dress.

"No, not for you." Maria shook her head. She contemplated the girls and wondered how much she ought to tell them. "Can you keep a secret?"

Consuelo clapped her hands. "I'm hot for secrets. Tell me one and you've told everyone, which saves a lot of wear and tear on your own mouth."

"Tonight I'm waiting for the boy I'm going to marry."

"So what's the secret?" Consuelo was disappointed. "You know something, Rosalia? Chino is all right. He doesn't talk as much as the others about what a great lover he is. And he doesn't talk big about going to work, because he goes to work. So you know what I figure?"

"What?" Rosalia asked patiently.

"He's a doer, not a talker—and they do the most in everything! When are you going to marry this great lover?"

Maria took a deep breath. "I am not waiting for Chino."

"Poor girl!" Consuelo placed her hand on Maria's forehead. "The heat's got her. She's way out of her mind."

"I am!" Maria's eyes danced with excitement. "I am out of my mind and out of this world with happiness. Tell me, do you think Chino could make me look like this?"

Puzzled, Consuelo looked to Rosalia for an explanation, but Rosalia shrugged. "I'll say this," Rosalia observed, "Maria does look different."

"I do?" Maria asked. "Even if I did not look different, can't you see that I feel different?"

Rosalia nodded. "Very different, like you were lit up with sparks."

"Which is how I feel!" Maria exclaimed. "I feel wonderful, marvelous and beautiful. I feel I could fly, if I wanted to. I could run along the edge of this roof and jump to that one." She pointed. "I only see stars in the sky. Four or five moons. I'm in love with the most wonderful, wonderful boy."

"Of course," Consuelo said. "Chino." She turned to her friend again. "He must really have something."

"A job," Rosalia snickered. "A big one."

"Oh shut up," Consuelo told her. "You are thinking practical and Maria is thinking romantical. I wonder . . . ?"

Rosalia shurgged. "She hasn't told us that part of the secret, so we can't broadcast it."

"But we can say she did—" Consuelo suggested.

Maria knelt to shut off the radio, then leaned over the side of the building. "Someone is calling me. Hello! We're up here, up on the roof." Joyously she turned to the girls. "Now you will see him!"

She ran to the door, held it open, and waited. Poor Tony, he must have knocked at the door, and found it locked.

"Up here!" she called. "Hurry! I want you to meet some friends of mine."

She paused and blinked because it was Chino on the landing below.

"I must talk to you," he called to Maria. "Who is up there with you?"

"The girls," Maria replied. "Chino, what is the matter? You look like you were in an accident!"

"Anita?" he asked.

"She's not here. Chino, you look sick," Maria said as she descended several steps. "What is the matter?"

Chino leaned against the wall, stared at his hands as if he had never seen them before, and wiped his streaked and sweaty face with the sleeve of his shirt. "Come down, Maria." He pointed to the other girls. "Stay where you are, don't listen."

"We don't have to be kicked out more than once to know when we're not wanted," Consuelo said to Chino.

"Let him alone!" Maria ran up the stairs to shut the roof door and returned to Chino. "What is it?" she asked. "You're in trouble?"

"Where're your father and mother? The kids?"

"They went to the movies. Chino, you've been fighting!"

Chino moaned, and covered his face with both hands. "It happened so fast."

"What happened so fast, Chino?"

"Maria, at the rumble—"

"There was no rumble," she said.

Chino turned from her. "There was. There was. Nobody meant for it to happen. Nobody." He pounded his fist against the painted plaster for emphasis.

Maria felt the cold breath of fear against her face.

"What is it?" she asked. "Tell me. Tell me fast. It will be easier if you say it very fast."

"There was a fight," Chino began, "and 'Nardo . . ."

"Go on."

"A knife . . ."

"Tony!" she shrieked as she whirled Chino around. "What happened to Tony?"

Eyes large with disbelief, Chino rested with one cheek against the wall. Then, for the first time, he saw that Maria wore the white dress and high-heeled shoes, even lipstick, and knew it was not for him.

"Tony?" He was savage. "He's all right. Fine! He just killed your brother!"

"You're lying. You're lying!" she said as she began to beat him with her fist. "You are making up a story, Chino, and I hate you! I will tell 'Nardo that you are not to come here any more. You are lying, lying, lying!" She paused at the sound of police siren. "Why do you lie?"

Pressed against the wall, Chino also heard the siren, and the shrill sound released him from the agony of the moment. He sprang forward and pushed Maria aside and ran downstairs to the flat, because he had work to do.

Not that 'Nardo or any of the Sharks had given him orders, but all of them would be looking for Tony Wyzek, and he—Chino Martin—had the most reason for finding him. And because 'Nardo had thought of him as a brother-in-law, 'Nardo had told him where he kept the gun. Chino reached behind the bathtub and felt the hard, compact package that Bernardo had concealed, and fear left him and he knew from this moment on he was an unfeeling extension of the trigger.

He unwrapped the gun and broke it to make certain it was loaded. The gun thrust into his pocket, Chino turned and pushed past a dazed Maria, who had just entered the apartment.

Now, he could see, she believed him, but there was no time for explanations, no time for anything but to find Tony Wyzek and kill him.

For a moment Maria thought of running after Chino, then she crossed the kitchen to kneel before the figures of the Holy Family, and looking directly at the Mother, she rocked in silent agony and prayer. She began to pray aloud in Spanish, attempting to remember every prayer she had ever heard or learned.

"Make it not be true," she pleaded. "I will do anything. Make me die. Only please—make it not be true."

Her prayers were interrupted by firm strong hands on her elbows, hands that wanted her to stand. It could not be, but she saw him and knew it was Tony, and he was no longer young. His eyes were old, sunk deep in his head, and his mouth twitched, as he breathed in deep, racking spasms.

Maria's hand struck him once, again, and again as she began to beat him with more violence than she had shown Chino. He made no effort to defend himself as her fists beat against his face. "Killer!" she wailed and moaned wildly, without stopping, "Killer killer killer killer—"

Suddenly she fell forward into Tony's arms, and together they slumped to the floor. Wet cheek pressed against his, she attempted to kiss away his tears, before she cradled him in her arms, where Tony wept with the anguish of the doomed.

"I tried to stop it. I did try," he cried brokenly. "I don't know how it went wrong. I didn't meant to hurt him. I swear it. I swear it. I didn't want to. But Riff—Riff was like my brother. So when Bernardo killed him . . ."

"God save them," she whispered.

Tony pulled Maria into his arms, began kissing her eyes, her cheeks, her hair, as he continued to pour out his grief.

"I had to tell you," he said. "I had to ask your forgiveness before I went to the police."

"No," she whispered. "No."

"It's easy now," Tony said. "I'm not afraid."

"No," she repeated wildly. "Stay with me. Stay with me. I'm alone. Stay with me."

He clasped her again in his arms, felt the warmth of her breasts, her hair, the tears against his cheeks. "I love you so much, Maria," he whispered. "And I killed someone you love. Help me—please help me."

"Hold me tighter," she answered. "Make your arms tighter. I am so cold."

How could there be any hours or days or future beyond tonight, beyond the moment when her mother and father returned from the movies?

"You must rest," she said. "On my bed. Anton, please."

"I've gotta go," he said.

"To the police?"

"To the police."

"After the rest." Maria stood and offered him both hands. "A little while ago I was talking to the girls on the roof about my wedding. And we were married, Anton. Don't you remember, this afternoon?"

"If we could only go back to the afternoon."

"It is afternoon. It will never be later for us. Now you must rest."

# • *CHAPTER EIGHT* •

Baby-John called on Superman, Batman and Robin, Wonder Boy and Planet King, Green Arrow and Green Hornet, Spaceman, Jack Blastoff, and Orbit Oscar to come to his rescue.

Sitting in the dark body of the wrecked truck, knees drawn to his chin, and eyes fixed on a star that he could see through a break in the metal side of the truck that rested on its axles in the junk yard near the river, he waited for a bright streak of light, like that of a meteor, marking the path made by one, possibly all of his heroes.

This was no ordinary signal for help that Baby-John was radaring to outer space, but a call that had to be heeded, for he had just seen two hard guys go down for the final count—Riff, whom he admired and wept for with affection, and Bernardo, whom he hated but also had to admire because he had proved himself a hard guy.

True, Tony Wyzek hadn't been a slouch—the way he had used the knife was artistry—but it was his fault that Riff and Bernardo were dead. Riff was eighteen, Bernardo about the same, Baby-John figured, and he was fourteen, which meant that if he ever succeeded in becoming as hard a character as Riff or Bernardo, he only had four years to live, maybe five. Which wasn't much time at all, especially if he might be spending two or three of the four or five years in the reformatory.

Only minutes before Baby-John had scaled one of the fences of the auto yard, wondered how far he could walk along the top, and decided to find out. With arms extended, fingers stiff, he moved slowly along the fence top so that his heroes, from Batman to Orbit Oscar, could see that he was worth saving. Baby-John sent them hard thoughts, because someone had better come get him before the cops did.

They had seen how he'd just got away from Schrank and Krupke—man, he had really spilled Krupke on his ass—but the cops would be bound to catch him eventually and Krupke would use the stick on him without mercy. A telephone pole was only inches from the end of the fence and Baby-John reached over to stand with his right foot on the cleats.

Suppose he left the yard, found Krupke and Schrank and tried to do them in with the icepick? Or suppose he just ran down Columbus Avenue and gave it to every man or boy PR over ten that he saw? What headlines he would get! But suppose he ran into—Tony Wyzek?

Baby-John held to the pole with both hands to keep from falling, he had become that dizzy. Would he kill Tony? Or was it his duty to defend Tony against the Sharks? Right now he needed leadership. If Batman and Robin wanted to find him it would be easy for they had X-ray eyes and hearing keen enough to tune in on his thoughts. But until his heroes came, he wanted someone up front in the Jets to tell him what to do.

Who'd asked the PR's to come here, Baby-John sobbed as he slid down the pole, looked around, and started toward the truck. Who'd asked them to come here and kill Riff, a really good guy?

"Anybody in there?" Baby-John whispered into the darkness of the truck. "This is Baby-John sending."

"Shut up and come in," A-Rab replied. "Over and out."

"It's good to be with someone," Baby-John sighed after he cleared his throat, wiped at his eyes and nose, and raised his grimy right hand in signal to any and all of his heroes, so that they would know where he was. "Krupke and Schrank—I came around a corner and there they were. For a second I thought it was all over for sure."

"All right." A-Rab was impatient. "You got a smoke? You know where some of the other guys are? You seen Tony?"

"Nobody has," Baby-John answered the last question and flipped his last cigarette to A-Rab, who was trembling as if he needed a fix. "I guess the other guys'll show up soon, I hope. Maybe they went home."

"Are you nuts?" A-Rab lit the cigarette and flicked the match at Baby-John. "That's where the cops're gonna look first. So don't you go home for at least a coupla days," he warned.

"I won't, A-Rab. Say, did you get a look at 'em?"

"Look at who?"

"Riff and Bernardo, after they got it. You know, there's lots of blood in people."

"Shut up!" A-Rab shuddered. "I'm gonna clout you one if you don't shut up."

"I'm only talking. Gee, I wish it was yesterday." Baby-John sighed. "Or tomorrow. Only there shouldn't've been a today. A-Rab, whad'ya say we run away?"

A-Rab slid to the floor of the truck and smoked with his head bowed low. "You're scared?"

"If you'll keep it a secret—yeah."

"Then you cut it out," A-Rab warned him. "You're making me scared and that scares me."

At the sound of a police siren in the black street outside the yard and the sound of running feet,

A-Rab dropped to the floor and Baby-John crouched in a corner where the shadow was deepest. A prowl car raced down the street and Baby-John was sure he heard a cop shout that he was going to use his gun if the runner didn't stop.

A-Rab crawled along the floor until he reached Baby-John. "What're we gonna do?"

"Wait here, I guess," Baby-John whispered. "That's what Action wants. Is he taking over?"

"I guess so," A-Rab replied. He twisted Baby-John's arm.

"Whatever happens, no deals with the cops? No tellin' them anything we know about tonight?"

"Nothing, I swear." Baby-John raised his hand. "The same movie is playing that I saw when them Sharks got me. So if I tell you about the action we've got us alibis."

A-Rab mussed the younger boy's hair. "Hey, you got a brain!"

"If we went to the movies what're we afraid of? Why're we hiding here?"

"Shut up and tell me about the movie," A-Rab said. "And make it interesting."

Caught up in the excitement of hiding from the police, the knowledge that he was no longer play acting, that A-Rab was depending on him, and that they were going to be told what to do by Action, who had never been afraid of anything, made Baby-John feel better and less dependent upon his heroes, busy elsewhere.

Suppose Action decided that they take over a roof, get a real arsenal up there, and see how long they could stand off the cops! Man, wouldn't that be a way to go out like a man! If Action didn't have a plan to get them out of this jam, standing off the cops was better than going to the reformatory. Baby-John could see it—cops all around, TV cameras and reporters all over the place, and there they'd be, up on the roof wearing gas masks so they couldn't be smoked out by gas.

"We gotta get gas masks," he said to A-Rab.

"Gas masks? What for?"

"To stand off the cops."

"What the hell're you talking about?"

"You'll see." Baby-John was cagey. "Things're gonna get worse because they'll be looking all over for us, like you said. So we gotta have some plan of action. So Action—I guess it's Action now?"

"Either him or Diesel," A-Rab agreed. "No, it's gotta be Action because he's got more up here." He touched his head. "At least I think—hope so. So Action is gonna have to tell us what to do."

"You think he can?" Baby-John was uncertain whether this made him feel good. If Action made the decisions, he would never get the chance to offer his plan. "Maybe he'll ask what we think."

"Maybe," A-Rab agreed and told Baby-John to be quiet because someone was whistling a signal. "That makes six guys who're here now," he said. "Not bad."

Gathered in the body of the truck, seated on cushions taken from other cars, they waited for more members of the Jets to show. Anybodys was talking her head off about the crowbar she had found which would be the greatest thing for prying open windows and doors, and could also serve as a weapon. But no one listened, for they were waiting impatiently for Action to finish his cigarette and tell them what to do.

Action counted heads—there were eight—no, nine Jets present, if he counted Anybodys—and ground his cigarette into the floor of the truck. "I guess we'd better get started," he said, "because I figure some of us must've got picked up. Now, are there any objections to my taking over?"

"Suits me," Mouthpiece said.

"Fine," Action continued after everyone had murmured that he was leader. "Who's got a plan?"

"I have," Anybodys said before Baby-John could speak. "We gotta save Tony. Because some certain parties are lookin' for him."

"So I say let'm find him and save us the trouble," Diesel said. "Action, don't you think we've had enough? We gotta get outa here before we're taken downtown for photographing with a number 'cross our chests. Certain parties are looking for Tony—I hope they find him. Dirty bastard." He spat. "If it wasn't for him Riff would be alive and I woulda taken Bernardo."

"Who's lookin' for Tony?" Action ignored Diesel.

Anybodys shifted to a part of the cushion through which the springs had not broken. "The Sharks," she said. "After everybody scattered, I figured I oughta infiltrate the PR territory. See what was goin' on. It doesn't take much of a shadow to hide me and I can move like nothin' most people ever saw."

"You *are* something most people never saw," Snowboy said. "So stop building and get on with it."

"You've got something to tell us?" Action asked Anybodys. "We're listening."

"I heard Chino talking to some of the Sharks. I was real close to them and they didn't know it." She could not resist the tone of accomplishment. "And he was telling them something about Tony and Bernardo's sister. Then he started to swear in spic but I understand a little." Again she paused. "Swore if it was the last thing he did, he was gonna get Tony."

"Tony'll knock his effen head off," Diesel said. "I mean the old Tony could."

"Could be," Anybodys agreed. "That's if Chino doesn't blow Tony apart first. I saw the gun he showed them."

"Goddamn them!" Action was on his feet. "Them lousy PR's don't let up! I don't wanna hear nothing outa you that sounds like double-crossing talk. I got no love for Tony, but if anybody fixes him it's us. No spics. Do I hear any objections?"

Standing before each of the Jets, Action moved on when he saw each of them move his head to signify that he was making the decisions, and like them or not, they were binding on all of them.

"We've gotta find him," Action said. "So we'll spread out. Anybodys, you think you can find Graziella and the other chicks?"

"I guess so," she said.

"Then tell them to look too. And whoever finds Tony brings him back here. So somebody's gotta stay. Somebody who's not afraid of being alone in the dark."

"That's me," Baby-John said.

"Then you stay. And if anybody shows give them the word. If Tony shows he stays here with you. Understand?"

"Sure." Baby-John nodded. "But maybe Any-bodys'll lend me her crowbar."

"If I get it back."

Action gestured for them to follow him from the truck, and as Baby-John settled himself with the crowbar at his side he began to send out hard thoughts again to his heroes.

A little sad, he wondered if his trouble was just too small for them to bother with. Maybe, on his way through outer space, Riff might put in a good word for him.

## • *CHAPTER NINE* •

Yes, she had kissed him as he lay on the bed, and in desperation he had clung to her, pressed his lips to her mouth. In anguished desperation he had grasped her, as if dying, and his right hand had touched her breast, hesitated, then with his palm cupped the warm flesh that beat under the fabric. And the knowledge that their lives together would be ended within minutes—at best within an hour or two—had compelled him to pull her over and across him, so that they were together on the bed.

He trembled again and attempted to leave the bed, so she had moved to the other pillow and listened as he wept, then slept. Soon her mother and father would be coming up the stairs—or were they on the way to the undertakers? Or would Bernardo be taken to the morgue?

She felt the bed shake as Tony trembled convulsively and drew up his legs as if in the throes of the bends. Groping through chaos, he gasped for breath and attempted to leave the bed.

"Stay," she said to him.

"Maria?" she heard him whisper, "Maria, I gotta go."

Not giving him time to speak again, she embraced him and fitted her breasts, her stomach, her loins to his body, and desire overcame fear, joy overcame sorrow, until a siren wailed in the street below.

Suddenly he thrust free and fumbled for his shoes. Terror rose in her throat and she pressed her lips against his cheek to keep the cry within her so that it would not escape to frighten the boy in whose arms she had lain.

"We are married," she sobbed. "This afternoon we were so happy. Tonight waiting for you I was so happy."

"You're young," he said. "You'll be happy again.

With someone better than me. That's what I see for you."

She shook her head. "Be my husband."

"I can't," he said. "I'm a murderer."

"Then be my lover."

"I can't." He turned away not to see her eyes. "Bernardo won't let me. My God, Maria, I killed him!"

"And he killed your friend. The boy who was like your brother."

"No." He had to deny it. "That was long ago. Just talk, nothing more. He was never my brother. At the end I don't even think he was my friend."

"To kill for him, he had to be more than a friend," she continued in her low, calm voice. "Tell me about him."

"What's there to tell?" He trembled with grief. "Riff was a good joe. He had guts, he wasn't afraid of anybody, and he was always looking for a fight to prove it."

Maria shook her head. "Like Bernardo."

"I guess so," Tony said. "The Jets meant a lot to him."

"Bernardo loved the Sharks."

"I guess they were alike."

Maria nodded as she sat on the bed and traced the damp outline of Tony's head on the pillow. She pitied Tony and Riff, who had been so like Bernardo. She had never seen Riff's eyes, but knew they had been like Bernardo's, ever restless and vicious, searching out hatreds as if to prove over and over again that he was a man, and always failing.

What future could there have been for Riff or Bernardo? None that she could see. In the warped years of their youth, they had seen, witnessed, found joy and participated in enough violences to age a dozen men. They loved nothing and destroyed everything, although they protested that it was one thing only that they hated—each other. So she pitied Riff as she pitied her brother, and would have willingly, at that moment, given her life for either of them.

But to what purpose? That they might kill other men? Eventually they had to die: in a bar or outside a poolroom, at some dance or in the back seat of an automobile, along a lonely stretch of highway or on some tenement roof. But not in bed. For boys like Riff and Bernardo preyed upon each other and were in turn preyed upon by every man and woman who could cater to and find profit in their violence. If they had lived to grow a little older, they would never grow wiser.

"That is why they both had to die," she said. "And that is why you must not. Because you were like them, once. But you wanted to be different—I know. And Riff and my poor brother did not."

"I don't understand," he said. "I killed Bernardo. Doesn't it mean anything that he was your brother? And that I did it to him?"

"You did not want to go there tonight," she said, speaking for sorrowing women everywhere. "I sent you. I made you promise to go."

"You did," he said quickly, to keep her from sharing any part of his guilt. "But you didn't want me to kill your brother. Don't you love him? Can't you cry for him?"

"Must you ask when I can cry for all the world? 'Nardo was my brother, and you are the man I love." She shook him. "I want to love everything in the world. Not only the things I know but the things and people I do not know and will never see or meet. Do you understand?"

"Look at us." He stared around the dark room, heavy with heat and shadows. "We've gone from living and loving to dying. It happened too fast."

A finger suddenly placed by Maria across his lips silenced him, and they heard the hard tap of high heels and Anita's frantic voice as she called out in the kitchen. "Maria?"

Anita knocked on the bedroom door. "Maria, it's Anita. Why are you locked in?"

Maria gestured for Tony to remain silent. "I didn't know it was locked."

"Open the door." Anita rattled the knob again. "I need you."

Tony placed his hand full across Maria's mouth. "Give me a second," he whispered. "Tell her to wait a second."

"One moment, Anita," Maria called. "I was asleep, and it is still in my eyes." She turned to Tony. "Where are you going?"

"To Doc's," he continued in a whisper. "If you'll go away with me, I'll wait there. You know where it is?"

"I walked by today to see if I could see you."

"He'll help us with money," Tony whispered as he stepped over the sill. "You'll meet me?"

Maria was silent as Anita tried the door again. "You're talking to someone," she called through the closed door. "Maria!"

"At Doc's." Maria placed a finger on Tony's lips. "As soon as I can." She watched Tony go quickly down the fire escape, then moved slowly toward the door. "Coming, Anita!"

Anita pushed by to look from the bed to the window to Bernardo's sister in her slip and bare feet.

"Did you see Chino?" Maria asked. "He was here before, and he was like a wild man." She paused because Anita continued to stare at her. "All right," she challenged Anita. "Now you know."

"You tramp!" Anita screamed and darted toward the window to slam it shut. "There isn't a whore in the world who would have done what you did! He killed your brother and you rewarded him by going to bed with him? What would you do if he killed your father and mother? Walk the streets for him?"

She was too spent, too tired to explain. She reached for Anita's hand, but Anita retreated to a corner of the room, to stare as if Maria were something so unclean, so ghoulish, she would never admit having seen her.

"I know what you're thinking," Maria said to the sobbing girl. "And he feels the same way."

"He should have died instead of his friend! Bernardo should have killed him!"

"Then Bernardo would have killed the boy I love."

Anita covered her ears. "I don't want to listen to you. Whore! I don't want to look at you!"

Maria walked slowly to the window to lean her forehead against the glass. The surface was cooler than the air in the room, and she wondered where Tony was now. Would he be able to evade the police and Bernardo's friends?

She wanted to tell Anita how she had felt; how, after Chino had told her of the murder, she had hated Tony, and how he had wanted to die.

"Chino has a gun," Anita said. "He's sending the boys out to find Tony."

"If he hurts Tony, touches him, I swear—"

"You'll do what Tony did to Bernardo?"

"I love Tony," she said simply.

Anita shook her head; nothing that had happened tonight could be comprehended. She had worn the Black Orchid, waited impatiently, looked at the first star and made a big wish. Now she would have to get a black dress for the funeral. "I know," she said to Maria. "I loved Bernardo."

Maria felt the color drain from her cheeks. "You must stay here until my mother and father come home. Someone must be here to tell them."

"And you can't?" Anita's laugh was scornful, acid with mockery. "Why not? It happens every day. Just tell them your brother is dead, murdered, and you're running away with the boy who killed their son."

"Try to understand," Maria pleaded.

"I can't!" Anita screamed. "I can't understand

and I don't want to because then I might understand . . ."

"You do," Maria said. "That is why you are
screaming. We are going away, Anita. I will meet
him at Doc's and if anyone tries to stop us they will
have to kill me too. You will tell that to Chino?"

The outside doorbell rang, then the door was thrust
open and the girls saw Schrank come in the kitchen.
Moving quickly, eyes taking in everything, he
opened the bathroom door, looked into the little
room, then looked into the other bedroom before
he closed the kitchen door and stood against it.
"I guess you know the news?" he said to Maria.
"You're his sister?"

"Yes. If you will tell me where to go to my brother . . ."

"He can wait." Schrank smiled at his wit.
"There're a couple of questions—"

"Later, please." Maria scooped her dress from the
bed and pulled it over her head. "I must go to him.
So please tell me."

"It'll only take a minute," Schrank said.

"Her brother's dead," Anita shrilled. "Couldn't
you wait until—"

"No!" His voice warned Anita to remain silent.
"You were at the center dance last night?"

"Yes." Maria nodded and gestured for Anita to
pull up the zipper in the back of her dress.

"Your brother got in a heavy argument because
you danced with someone he didn't like." Schrank
watched the girls closely. It was going to be very
tough on him if he didn't break this quickly. "You

want to see Bernardo? Fine, I'll take you and on the way you can start telling me what you know."

"Excuse me, Anita, my headache is worse," Maria said. "Will you go to the drugstore, for—how do you call it?"

"Aspirin," Anita replied, but made no sign that she would go. Schrank indicated the bathroom and kitchen cabinets. "Don't you keep aspirin around here?"

"The bottle is empty," Maria replied. "Will you go for me, Anita? Please? Otherwise they might close the store."

"We've got aspirin where we're going," Schrank took Maria's arm.

"Will I be long?"

Schrank shrugged as he looked at his wristwatch. "As long as it takes."

"I won't be long," Maria said and turned from Schrank so that he could not see how her eyes pleaded with Anita. "You could wait for me at the drugstore? I won't be long."

"I'll wait. And maybe Doc will stay open for you," Anita replied. She turned to Schrank. "Don't you do anything rough with this girl. She has suffered enough tonight. And I am 'Nardo's girl." She was defiant.

"Were," Schrank corrected her.

"Please, you wanted to ask me questions," Maria said to distract Schrank.

"Not ask." Schrank followed her down the tenement stairs and crinkled his nose at the foreign odors. "I'm telling you. There was an argument over a boy."

"Another from my country," she said without hesitation.

"What's his name?"

She looked up at Schrank. "Jose."

A block from the drugstore Anita combed her hair and wiped her face with a damp handkerchief, which she threw away. Without using a mirror she renewed her lipstick, then smoothed the skirt of her dress, for she was in America where the Americans mourned quietly, as if ashamed of showing sorrow, and she was as capable as any of them.

Only after she entered the drugstore did she hesitate, for the doors of both phone booths folded back and A-Rab and Diesel stared at her in tight-lipped silence.

"I'd like to see Doc," she said slowly.

A-Rab looked at Diesel before shaking his head. "He ain't here."

"Where is he?" she asked as her eyes darted toward the door behind the prescription counter.

"He's gone to the bank." A-Rab picked at his teeth. "There was an error in his favor."

"Very funny," she said. "Especially since banks are closed at night. Now where is he?"

"At the bank," Diesel said. "You know how skinny Doc is. He slipped in through the night deposit slot."

"And got stuck in halfways assways," A-Rab

agreed, as he left the phone booth. "Which indicates there's no telling when he'll get back."

He opened the front door, bowed, and pointed to the street. *"Buenas noches, señorita.* Maybe you can earn a coupla bucks on the way home." He slammed the door and ran after Anita and grabbed her just as she reached the counter. "Where you think you're goin'?"

"Back there." She struggled to free herself. "I want to see Doc."

"If you're knocked up come back tomorrow," Diesel said as he moved behind the counter to block the door. "You deaf?" he asked. "We told you he ain't here."

"I hear as well as you," she insisted and felt the heat of color darken her cheeks. These boys were dangerous, and she didn't like the way their eyes concentrated on her breasts, which she now wished were smaller and restrained by an ordinary brassiere. "I want to see for myself."

"Say please." Diesel's suggestion was a warning.

"Please. Now will you let me pass, please?"

A-Rab stood on his toes, the better to look down her dress. "You're too dark to pass. Hey, that's some bra you're not wearing."

"You're dirty," she said.

"You're stacked like—what do they build them out of in Puerto Rico?" A-Rab laughed.

Anita trembled and gripped her purse to use it as a weapon. "Don't," she warned them, her voice low.

*"Please* don't," Diesel corrected her and winked at A-Rab to continue his harassment, because

A-Rab could be awfully funny once he got started. *"Please* don't."

*"Por favor,"* A-Rab mocked her. "You *non comprende,* spic?" He laughed and stood on his toes again. "Spic, you no spick English? Too bad. So first I'll teach you all the dirty words."

"Listen you, I've got to give a friend of yours a message. I've got to tell Tony . . ."

". . . who isn't here." Diesel was sharp and gestured for A-Rab to lay off for a moment. "Now blow."

"I know he is. Never mind who the message is from," she appealed to Diesel. "Let me give it to Tony."

"Why not give it to me?" A-Rab asked as he pinned her against a row of shelves and began to grind away at her. "How's this for a mambo-Ai! movement?"

"Get away from me." She tried to hit him. "Pig!" A-Rab tore the purse from her hand and threw it aside. "I want to stop Chino! Stop doing that, you pig!"

"You're the pig," A-Rab grunted. "You're Bernardo's tramp, you goddamn garlic mouth, gold tooth, pierced ear lyin' pig. If you think you're gonna set up Tony for Chino you've got other work cut out for you."

Suddenly A-Rab pinned Anita's arm and tripped her. She fell behind the counter and he felt how her leg muscles tightened as he began to rotate his belly against her as his free hands tore at her dress.

"Get her, A-Rab!" Diesel whooped. "Show her how an American rides! Let her tell that to Chino!"

"Relax, baby." A-Rab slapped at Anita. "You're gonna be raped so why don't you relax and enjoy . . ."

A-Rab felt two hands tugging at his shirt and heard Diesel tell him to let up. "It's Doc, he just come upstairs."

Reluctantly, breathing heavily, A-Rab stood and permitted Anita to stand. She saw Doc staring at her, mouth agape, then heard him turn to shout at the boys that they were lice, worse than lice, and they were going to pay for what they had done.

"Are you all right?" Doc asked.

She bit at her lips and held together the torn front of her dress. "Bernardo was right." She fought to hold back the tears as she looked at A-Rab, who was picking at his teeth. "If one of you was bleeding in the street I'd walk by and spit on you."

"Go home." Doc's advice was gentle.

"Don't let her go! She'll tell Chino that Tony . . ." A-Rab pushed by Doc and started for the door. "She's not getting outa here!"

She struck out at Diesel and A-Rab. "I'll give you the message for your American buddy! Tell the murderer that Maria's never going to meet him!" Her laughter was full, triumphant, as she saw Diesel and A-Rab stand aside. "Tell him Chino found out about them—and shot her!"

The door slammed behind Anita and Doc collapsed against the counter. "God help me, I must tell him. Get out of here!" he shouted at Diesel and

A-Rab. "Get out and see if you can find a church someplace that doesn't lock its doors against you!"

Diesel nudged A-Rab. "I'm clearing out."

"Where to?"

"You name it," Diesel said at the door. "As long as it's north, south, or west of here."

## • *CHAPTER TEN* •

He ran from the pharmacy in anguish, without direction or hope. She was gone, and she would never return. His guilt had bred other guilt and the job wasn't finished; Chino still had work to do.

He didn't know what Chino had planned, but he knew what he planned for Chino. He would find Chino and Chino would have to kill him.

It was the only way to end this, and he was impatient for the end because he no longer wanted to live.

There were people on the streets and as he strode rapidly along the sidewalks, he heard the people on the stoops, the sidewalks, and as they leaned against automobiles, heard them talking about everything and nothing.

The black and white design of a police prowl car made him dart into a hallway and when the car passed him, he hurried toward the Coffee Pot but Chino wasn't there. Then he realized that he could never find Chino on the streets, that he would have to take to the backyards, the cellars or the roofs. He would have to let Chino know that he was hunting instead of being hunted.

"Chino?" He stood in the yard between two tenements in PR territory and called loud enough to be heard. Then he took a deep breath and bellowed. "Come and get me, Chino! I'm waiting!"

He heard a movement, whirled toward it, and spread his arms wide to make himself a full target. But the voice that called his name was not Chino's, and in the dim light he saw Anybodys running toward him. "You're crazy!" she challenged him. "This is PR territory."

"Get out of here." He brushed Anybodys aside, before he cupped his hands to shout again. "Chino —come get me! Damn you—I'm waiting!"

Anybodys clung to his arm and tried to pull him toward the cellar. "The gang—"

"Beat it! I'm warning you." He swung his right hand in a full arc and his open palm caught Anybodys across the face. Above him the lights went on in several windows, and Tony ran toward the end of the yard. "Chino!" he shouted. "Where the hell are you, Chino? I'm waiting for you. Hurry up and—"

The bullet struck him full in the chest and whirled him around in a confusion of pain and sound, and as the blood rose to his mouth, he thought he saw a white figure running toward him and calling his name.

Maria flung herself on the body that lay face upward, and her tears spilled over to wet the lifeless cheeks of Tony Wyzek, who had died with the roar of the city in his ears, had died too young to have it really said that he had ever lived. She raised herself from the body, but covered Tony's eyes with her hand, and as she saw Anybodys walking toward her, very slowly, she ordered the girl to stop.

"Stay back," she warned Chino too. "No, come over here and give me the gun."

She felt the hard, cruel metal in her hand, realized how easily and well it fitted the grip. "How do you fire this?" she asked Chino. "Just by pulling this little trigger?"

She saw Chino shrink as she raised the gun, to point its muzzle at him. "How many bullets are left, Chino? Enough for you? And you?" She pointed the gun at Anybodys, who stood against the side of the building. "We all killed him. My brother and Riff and I killed him. Not Chino!"

She held him with the gun. "Can I kill you, Chino? And will there be a bullet left for me?"

She felt a hand on her shoulder, a gentle voice in her ear, recognized the face of Doc. He told her that together they would go to Tony's mother, for she had to be told, and she would need the comfort of another woman, especially one who had loved her son.

If ten streets and ten thousand people, even

twenty, thirty thousand, knew of the tragedy, the other millions of people and the tens of thousands of streets in New York did not. Some, not many of the papers, carried a headline about the murders under the highway, but the details were scanty and incomplete.

But most of the people in the city slept or had a good time, because it was Saturday night, the one night in the week when a man just had to let go. There were people who loved, who ate, who lusted and promoted. There were people who died in peace, in pain and in violence.

And there were people who looked up at the sky and ached with loneliness, as they appealed in silence to the stars and the moon. They hoped that someplace, somewhere, someone heard them, that their own little dreams would come true, that very soon they would meet someone they could trust, could love and be happy with.

Some of the wishes came true, but it made no difference to the city because it had been built to endure beyond the lifetime of all the people that inhabited it.

That is the way things were. And if things did not change, the way it would always be.